THE VOYAGES OF
DOCTOR DOLITTLE
and Other Tales
by
HUGH LOFTING

Illustrations by the author

Selected and Edited

SCHOLASTIC INC.
New York Toronto London Auckland Sydney

ISBN 0-590-33133-7

12 11 10 9 8 7 6 5 4 3 2   5 6 7/8

Printed in the U.S.A.   11

Contents

The Story of
DOCTOR DOLITTLE

Puddleby

ONCE UPON A TIME, many years ago — when our grandfathers were little children — there was a doctor, and his name was Dolittle — John Dolittle, M.D. "M.D." means that he was a proper doctor and knew a whole lot.

He lived in a little town called Puddleby-on-the-Marsh. All the folks, young and old, knew him well by sight. And whenever he walked down the street in his high hat, everyone would say, "There goes the Doctor! — He's a clever man." And the dogs and the children would all run up and follow behind him; and even the crows that lived in the church tower would caw and nod their heads.

The house he lived in, on the edge of the town, was quite small; but his garden was very large, and had a wide lawn and stone seats and weeping willows hanging over. His sister, Sarah Dolittle, was housekeeper for him; but the Doctor looked after the garden himself.

He was very fond of animals and kept many kinds of pets. Besides the goldfish in the pond at the bottom of his garden, he had rabbits in the pantry, white mice in his piano, a squirrel in the linen closet, and a hedgehog in the cellar. He had a cow with a calf too, and an old lame horse — twenty-five years of age — and chickens, and pigeons, and two lambs, and many other animals. But his favorite pets were Dab-Dab the duck, Jip the dog, Gub-Gub the baby pig, Polynesia the parrot, and the owl Too-Too.

His sister used to grumble about all these animals, and said they made the house untidy. And one day when an old lady with rheumatism came to see the Doctor, she sat on the hedgehog, who was sleeping on the sofa, and never came to see him any more, but drove every Saturday all the way to Oxenthorpe, another town ten miles off, to see a different doctor.

Then his sister, Sarah Dolittle, came to him and said,

"John, how can you expect sick people to come and see you when you keep all these animals in the house? It's a fine doctor would have his parlor full of hedgehogs and mice! That's the fourth personage these animals have driven away. Squire Jenkins and the Parson say they wouldn't come near your house again — no matter how sick they are. We are getting poorer every day. If you go on like this, none of the best people will have you for a doctor."

"But I like the animals better than the 'best people,' " said the Doctor.

"You are ridiculous," said his sister, and walked out of the room.

So, as time went on, the Doctor got more and more animals, and the people who came to see him got less and less. Till at last he had no one left — except the Cat's Meat Man, who didn't mind any kind of animals. But the Cat's Meat Man wasn't very rich and he only got sick once a year — at Christmastime, when he used to give the Doctor sixpence for a bottle of medicine.

Sixpence a year wasn't enough to live on — even

in those days, long ago; and if the Doctor hadn't had some money saved up in his moneybox, no one knows what would have happened.

And he kept on getting still more pets, and of course it cost a lot to feed them. And the money he had saved up grew littler and littler.

Then he sold his piano, and let the mice live in a bureau drawer. But the money he got for that too began to go, so he sold the brown suit he wore on Sundays and went on becoming poorer and poorer.

And now, when he walked down the street in his high hat, people would say to one another, "There goes John Dolittle, M.D.! There was a time when he was the best-known doctor in the West Country — Look at him now — He hasn't any money, and his stockings are full of holes!"

But the dogs and the cats and the children still ran up and followed him through the town — the same as they had done when he was rich.

Animal Language

I T HAPPENED ONE DAY that the Doctor was sitting
in his kitchen talking with the Cat's Meat Man,
who had come to see him with a stomachache.

"Why don't you give up being a people's doctor
and be an animal doctor?" asked the Cat's Meat
Man.

The parrot, Polynesia, was sitting in the window looking out at the rain and singing a sailor song to herself. She stopped singing and started to listen.

"You see, Doctor," the Cat's Meat Man went on, "you know all about animals — much more than what these here vets do. That book you wrote about cats, why, it's wonderful! I can't read or write myself, or maybe *I'd* write some books. But my wife, Theodosia, she's a scholar, she is. And she read your book to me. Well, it's wonderful — that's all can be said — wonderful. You might have been a cat yourself. You know the way they think. And listen: you can make a lot of money doctoring animals. Do you know that? You see, I'd send all the old women who had sick cats or dogs to you. And if they didn't get sick fast enough, I could put something in the meat I sell 'em to make 'em sick, see?"

"Oh no," said the Doctor quickly. "You mustn't do that. That wouldn't be right."

"Oh, I didn't mean real sick," answered the Cat's Meat Man. "Just a little something to make them droopy-like was what I had reference to. But as you say, maybe it ain't quite fair on the animals. But they'll get sick anyway, because the old women always give 'em too much to eat. And look, all the farmers round about who had lame horses and weak lambs — they'd come. Be an animal doctor."

When the Cat's Meat Man had gone, the parrot flew off the window onto the Doctor's table and said,

"That man's got sense. That's what you ought to do. Be an animal doctor. Give the silly people up, if they haven't brains enough to see you're the best doctor in the world. Take care of animals instead — they'll soon find it out. Be an animal doctor."

"Oh, there are plenty of animal doctors," said John Dolittle, putting the flowerpots outside on the window sill to get the rain.

"Yes, there *are* plenty," said Polynesia. "But none of them are any good at all. Now listen, Doctor, and I'll tell you something. Did you know that animals can talk?"

"I knew that parrots can talk," said the Doctor.

"Oh, we parrots can talk in two languages — people's language and bird language," said Polynesia proudly. "If I say, 'Polly wants a cracker,' you understand me. But hear this: *'Ka-ka oi-ee, fee-fee?'*"

13

"Good gracious!" cried the Doctor. "What does that mean?"

"That means, 'Is the porridge hot yet?' — in bird language."

"My! You don't say so!" said the Doctor. "You never talked that way to me before."

"What would have been the good?" said Polynesia, dusting some cracker crumbs off her left wing. "You wouldn't have understood me if I had."

"Tell me some more," said the Doctor, all excited; and he rushed over to the dresser drawer and came back with the butcher's book and a pencil. "Now don't go too fast, and I'll write it down. This is interesting — very interesting — something quite new. Give me the birds' ABC first — slowly now."

So that was the way the Doctor came to know that animals had a language of their own and could talk to one another. And all that afternoon, while it was raining, Polynesia sat on the kitchen table giving him bird words to put down in the book.

At teatime, when the dog Jip came in, the parrot said to the Doctor, "See, *he's* talking to you."

"Looks to me as though he were scratching his ear," said the Doctor.

"But animals don't always speak with their

14

mouths," said the parrot in a high voice, raising her eyebrows. "They talk with their ears, with their feet, with their tails — with everything. Sometimes they don't *want* to make a noise. Do you see now the way he's twitching up one side of his nose?"

"What's that mean?" asked the Doctor.

"That means, 'Can't you see that it's stopped raining?' " Polynesia answered. "He is asking you a question. Dogs nearly always use their noses for asking questions."

After a while, with the parrot's help, the Doctor got to learn the language of the animals so well that he could talk to them himself and understand everything they said. Then he gave up being a people's doctor altogether.

As soon as the Cat's Meat Man had told everyone that John Dolittle was going to become an animal doctor, old ladies began to bring him their pet pugs and poodles who had eaten too much cake, and farmers came many miles to show him sick cows and sheep.

One day a plow horse was brought to him, and the poor thing was terribly glad to find a man who could talk in horse language.

"You know, Doctor," said the horse, "that vet

over the hill knows nothing at all. He has been treating me six weeks now — for spavins. What I need is *spectacles*. I am going blind in one eye. There's no reason why horses shouldn't wear glasses, the same as people. But that stupid man over the hill never even looked at my eyes. He kept on giving me big pills. I tried to tell him, but he couldn't understand a word of horse language. What I need is spectacles."

"Of course — of course," said the Doctor. "I'll get you some at once."

"I would like a pair like yours," said the horse — "only green. They'll keep the sun out of my eyes while I'm plowing the Fifty-Acre Field."

"Certainly," said the Doctor. "Green ones you shall have."

"You know, the trouble is, Sir," said the plow horse as the Doctor opened the front door to let him out — "the trouble is that *anybody* thinks he can doctor animals — just because the animals don't complain. As a matter of fact it takes a much cleverer man to be a really good animal doctor than it does to be a people's doctor. My farmer's boy thinks he knows all about horses. I wish you could see him — his face is so fat he looks as though he had no eyes, and he has got as much brain as a potato bug. He tried to put a mustard plaster on me last week."

"Where did he put it?" asked the Doctor.

"Oh, he didn't put it anywhere — on me," said the horse. "He only tried to. I kicked him into the duck pond."

"Well, well!" said the Doctor.

"I'm a pretty quiet creature as a rule," said the horse — "very patient with people — don't make much fuss. But it was bad enough to have that vet giving me the wrong medicine. And when that red-faced booby started to monkey with me, I just couldn't bear it any more."

"Did you hurt the boy much?" asked the Doctor.

"Oh no," said the horse. "I kicked him in the right place. The vet's looking after him now. When will my glasses be ready?"

"I'll have them for you next week," said the Doctor. "Come in again Tuesday. Good morning!"

Then John Dolittle got a fine big pair of green spectacles, and the plow horse stopped going blind in one eye and could see as well as ever.

And soon it became a common sight to see farm animals wearing glasses in the country round Puddleby; and a blind horse was a thing unknown.

And so, in a few years' time, every living thing

17

for miles and miles got to know about John Dolittle, M.D. And the birds who flew to other countries in the winter told the animals in foreign lands of the wonderful doctor of Puddleby-on-the-Marsh, who could understand their talk and help them in their troubles. In this way he became famous among the animals all over the world — better known even than he had been among the folks of the West Country. And he was happy, and liked his life very much.

One afternoon when the Doctor was busy writing in a book, Polynesia sat in the window — as she nearly always did — looking out at the leaves blowing about in the garden.

The Doctor looked up and said, "How old are you, Polynesia? I know that parrots and elephants sometimes live to be very, very old."

"I can never be quite sure of my age," said Polynesia. "It's either a hundred and eighty-three or a hundred and eighty-two. But I know that when I first came here from Africa, King Charles was still hiding in the oak tree — because I saw him. He looked scared to death."

More Money Troubles

AND SOON NOW the Doctor began to make money again, and his sister Sarah bought a new dress and was happy.

Some of the animals who came to see him were so sick that they had to stay at the Doctor's house for a week. And when they were getting better, they used to sit in chairs on the lawn.

And often, even after they got well, they did not want to go away — they liked the Doctor and his house so much. And he never had the heart to refuse them when they asked if they could stay with him. So in this way he went on getting more and more pets.

Once when he was sitting on his garden wall, smoking a pipe in the evening, an organ grinder came round with a monkey on a string. The Doctor saw at once that the monkey's collar was too tight and that he was dirty and unhappy. So he took the monkey away from the organ grinder, gave the man a shilling, and told him to go. The organ grinder got awfully angry and said that he wanted to keep the monkey. But the Doctor told him that if he didn't go, he would punch him on the nose. John Dolittle was a strong man, though he wasn't very tall. So the man went away saying rude things, and the monkey stayed with Doctor Dolittle and had a good home. The other animals in the house called him "Chee-Chee," which is a common word in monkey language, meaning "ginger."

And another time, when the circus came to Puddleby, the crocodile, who had a bad toothache, escaped at night and came into the Doctor's garden.

The Doctor talked to him in crocodile language and took him into the house and made his tooth better. But when the crocodile saw what a nice house it was — with all the different places for the different kinds of animals — he too wanted to live with the Doctor. He asked couldn't he sleep in the fish pond at the bottom of the garden, if he promised not to eat the fish. When the circus men came to take him back, he got so wild and savage that he frightened them away. But to everyone in the house he was always as gentle as a kitten.

But now the old ladies grew afraid to send their lap dogs to Doctor Dolittle because of the crocodile, and the farmers wouldn't believe that he would not eat the lambs and sick calves they brought to be cured. So the Doctor went to the crocodile and told him he must go back to the circus. But he wept such big tears, and begged so hard to be allowed to stay, that the Doctor hadn't the heart to turn him out.

So then the Doctor's sister came to him and said, "John, you must send that creature away. Now the farmers and the old ladies are afraid to send their animals to you — just as we were beginning to be well off again. Now we shall be ruined entirely.

This is the last straw. I will no longer be house-keeper for you if you don't send away that alligator."

"It isn't an alligator," said the Doctor — "It's a crocodile."

"I don't care what you call it," said his sister. "It's a nasty thing to find under the bed. I won't have it in the house."

"But he has promised me," the Doctor answered, "that he will not bite anyone. He doesn't like the circus, and I haven't the money to send him back to Africa where he comes from. He minds his own business, and on the whole is very well behaved. Don't be so fussy."

"I tell you I *will not* have him around," said Sarah. "He eats the linoleum. If you don't send him away this minute I'll — I'll go and get married!"

"All right," said the Doctor, "go and get married. It can't be helped." And he took his hat and went out into the garden.

So Sarah Dolittle packed her things and went off, and the Doctor was left all alone with his animal family.

And very soon he was poorer than he had ever been before. With all these mouths to fill, and the house to look after, and no one to do the mending, and no money coming in to pay the butcher's bill, things began to look very difficult. But the Doctor didn't worry at all.

"Money is a nuisance," he used to say. "We'd all be much better off if it had never been invented. What does money matter, so long as we are happy?"

But Too-Too the owl, who was good at arithmetic, figured out that there was only money enough left to last another week — if they each had one meal a day and no more.

Then the animals made a vegetable and flower stall outside the garden gate and sold radishes and roses to the people that passed by along the road.

But still they didn't seem to make enough money to pay all the bills — and still the Doctor didn't worry.

He didn't even worry when Chee-Chee the monkey came to him panting and badly out of breath.

"Doctor!" he cried. "I've just had a message from a cousin of mine in Africa. There is a terrible sickness among the monkeys out there. They are all catching it, and they are dying in hundreds."

"Dear me!" said the Doctor. "Then we shall just have to go to Africa."

"But that takes money," said Dab-Dab, who was always practical about such things.

"Well, well," murmured the Doctor. "Never mind. Perhaps if I go down to the seaside I shall be able to borrow a boat that will take us to Africa. I knew a seaman once who brought his baby to me with measles. Maybe he'll lend me his boat — the baby got well."

So early the next morning the Doctor went down to the seashore. And when he came back he told the animals it was all right — the sailor was going to lend them the boat.

The sailor even borrowed enough food for them to stock the ship for the journey, and the Doctor and his whole family went off to Africa.

Although the ship was wrecked in a bad storm on the coast of Africa, they all got ashore safely.

It didn't take Doctor Dolittle long to cure the monkeys of their sickness, and they were so grateful they wanted to give him a going-away present. They asked Chee-Chee what the Doctor would like.

"Why not give him a rare animal," suggested Chee-Chee. "He could then charge people to see it and never have to be without money again."

And the chief of the monkeys asked, "Have they an iguana over there?"

"Yes, there is one in the London Zoo," replied Chee-Chee.

And another asked, "Have they an okapi?"

But Chee-Chee said, "Yes, in Belgium, where my organ grinder took me five years ago, they have an okapi in a big city they call Antwerp."

And another asked, "Have they a pushmi-pullyu?"

Then Chee-Chee said, "No. No white man has ever seen a pushmi-pullyu. Let us give him that."

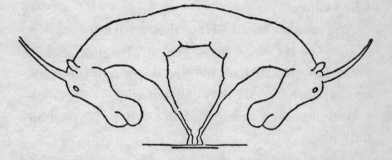

The Rarest Animal of All

PUSHMI-PULLYUS are now extinct. That means, there aren't any more. But long ago, when Doctor Dolittle was alive, there were some of them still left in the deepest jungles of Africa; and even then they were very, very scarce. They had no tail, but a head at each end and sharp horns on each head. They were very shy and terribly hard to catch. The natives get most of their animals by sneaking up behind them while they are not looking. But you could not do this with the pushmi-pullyu, because no matter which way you came toward him, he was always facing you. And besides, only one half of him slept at a time. The other head was always awake — and watching. This was why they were never caught and never seen in zoos. Though many of the greatest huntsmen and the cleverest menagerie keepers spent years of their lives searching through the jungles in all weathers for pushmi-pullyus, not a single one had ever been caught. Even then, years ago, he was the only animal in the world with two heads.

Well, the monkeys set out hunting for this animal through the forest. And after they had gone a good many miles, one of them found peculiar footprints near the edge of a river; and they knew that a pushmi-pullyu must be very near the spot.

Then they went along the bank of the river a little way and they saw a place where the grass was high and thick; and they guessed that he was in there.

So they all joined hands and made a great circle round the high grass. The pushmi-pullyu heard them coming, and he tried hard to break through the ring of monkeys. But he couldn't do it. When he saw that it was no use trying to escape, he sat down and waited to see what they wanted.

They asked him if he would go with Doctor Dolittle and be put on show in the Land of the White Men.

But he shook both his heads hard and said, "Certainly not!"

They explained to him that he would not be shut up in a menagerie but would just be looked at. They told him that the Doctor was a very kind man, but hadn't any money; and people would pay to see a two-headed animal, and the Doctor would get rich and could pay for the boat he had borrowed to come to Africa in.

But he answered, "No. You know how shy I am — I hate being stared at." And he almost began to cry.

Then for three days they tried to persuade him.

And at the end of the third day he said he would come with them and see what kind of a man the Doctor was, first.

So the monkeys traveled back with the pushmi-pullyu. And when they came to where the Doctor's little house of grass was, they knocked on the door.

The duck, who was packing the trunk, said, "Come in!"

And Chee-Chee very proudly took the animal inside and showed him to the Doctor.

"What in the world is it?" asked John Dolittle, gazing at the strange creature.

"Lord save us!" cried the duck. "How does it make up its mind?"

"It doesn't look to me as though it had any," said Jip the dog.

"This, Doctor," said Chee-Chee, "is the pushmi-pullyu — the rarest animal of the African jungles, the only two-headed beast in the world! Take him home with you and your fortune's made. People will pay any money to see him."

"But I don't want any money," said the Doctor.

"Yes, you do," said Dab-Dab the duck. "Don't you remember how we had to pinch and scrape to pay the butcher's bill in Puddleby? And how are you going to get the sailor the new boat you spoke of unless we have the money to buy it?"

"I was going to make him one," said the Doctor.

"Oh, do be sensible!" cried Dab-Dab. "Where would you get all the wood and the nails to make one with? And besides, what are we going to live on? We shall be poorer than ever when we get back. Chee-Chee's perfectly right: take the funny-looking thing along, do!"

"Well, perhaps there is something in what you say," murmured the Doctor. "It certainly would make a nice new kind of pet. But does the — er — what-do-you-call-it really want to go abroad?"

"Yes, I'll go," said the pushmi-pullyu, who saw at once, from the Doctor's face, that he was a man to be trusted. "You have been so kind to the animals here — and the monkeys tell me that I am the only one who will do. But you must promise me that if I do not like it in the Land of the White Men you will send me back."

"Why, certainly — of course, of course," said the Doctor. "Excuse me, surely you are related to the Deer Family, are you not?"

"Yes," said the pushmi-pullyu — "to the Abyssinian gazelles and the Asiatic chamois — on my mother's side. My father's great-grandfather was the last of the unicorns."

"Most interesting!" murmured the Doctor; and he took a book out of the trunk which Dab-Dab was packing and began turning the pages. "Let us see if Buffon says anything — "

"I notice," said the duck, "that you only talk with one of your mouths. Can't the other head talk as well?"

"Oh yes," said the pushmi-pullyu. "But I keep the other mouth for eating — mostly. In that way

I can talk while I am eating without being rude. Our people have always been very polite."

When the packing was finished, and everything was ready to start, the monkeys gave a grand party for the Doctor, and all the animals of the jungle came. And they had pineapples and mangoes and honey and all sorts of good things to eat and drink.

After they had all finished eating, the Doctor got up and said,

"My friends: I am not clever at speaking long words after dinner, like some men; and I have just eaten many fruits and much honey. But I wish to tell you that I am very sad at leaving your beautiful country. Because I have things to do in the Land of the White Men, I must go. After I have gone, remember never to let the flies settle on your food before you eat it; and do not sleep on the ground when the rains are coming. I — er — er — I hope you will all live happily ever after."

When the Doctor stopped speaking and sat down, all the monkeys clapped their hands a long time and said to one another, "Let it be remembered always among our people that he sat and ate with us, here, under the trees. For surely he is the Greatest of Men!"

And the Grand Gorilla, who had the strength of seven horses in his hairy arms, rolled a great rock up to the head of the table and said, "This stone for all time shall mark the spot."

And even to this day, in the heart of the jungle, that stone still is there. And monkey mothers, passing through the forest with their families, still point down at it from the branches and whisper to their children, "Sh! There it is — look — where the Good White Man sat and ate food with us in the Year of the Great Sickness!"

Then, when the party was over, the Doctor and his pets started out to go back to the seashore. And all the monkeys went with him as far as the edge of their country, carrying his trunk and bags, to see him off.

The Voyages of
DOCTOR DOLITTLE

The Doctor's Kitchen

MY NAME IS TOMMY STUBBINS. I was just nine and a half years old when I first met the famous Doctor Dolittle.

I had found an injured squirrel. I asked Matthew Mugg, the Cat's Meat Man, who could help it, and he said, "Only one man: Doctor Dolittle!"

By luck, I shortly ran into the great man himself. There was a terrible storm, and hurrying along with our heads down, we ran into each other and knocked each other flat onto the wet pavement. Instead of being angry, the Doctor laughed and insisted on taking me to his own house to dry off.

The dark hallway of the Doctor's house seemed to be filled with animals. They bumped and pushed against me and made a tremendous noise.

"Don't be alarmed," he said. "These are just some of my pets. I've been away three months and they are glad to see me home again."

And then I thought I really must be dreaming! For there, craning her neck round the bend of the landing, hopping down the stairs on one leg, came a spotless white duck. And in her right foot she carried a lighted candle!

When at last I could look around me I found that the hall was indeed simply full of animals. It seemed to me that almost every kind of creature from the countryside must be there: a pigeon, a white mouse, an owl, a badger, a jackdaw — there was even a small pig, just in from the rainy garden, carefully wiping his feet on the mat while the light from the candle glistened on his wet pink back.

The Doctor took the candlestick from the duck and turned to me.

"Look here," he said, "you must get those wet clothes off. By the way, what is your name?"

"Tommy Stubbins," I said.

"Oh, are you the son of Jacob Stubbins, the shoe-maker?"

"Yes," I said.

"Excellent bootmaker, your father," said the Doctor. "You see these?" and he held up his right foot to show me the enormous boots he was wearing. "Your father made those boots four years ago, and I've been wearing them ever since — perfectly wonderful boots. Well now, look here, Stubbins. You've got to change those wet things — and quick. Wait a moment till I get some more candles lit, and then we'll go upstairs and find some dry clothes. You'll have to wear an old suit of mine till we can get yours dry again by the kitchen fire."

We changed to two suits of the Doctor's and as soon as we had a huge fire blazing up the chimney we hung our wet clothes around on chairs.

"You'll stay and have supper with me, Stubbins, of course?"

Already I was beginning to be very fond of this

funny little man who called me "Stubbins," instead of "Tommy" or "little lad." (I did so hate to be called "little lad"!) This man seemed to begin right away treating me as though I were a grown-up friend of his. And when he asked me to stop and have supper with him I felt terribly proud and happy.

"Thank you very much. I would like to stay," I replied.

"Did you see where I put my bag?" asked the Doctor.

"I think it is still in the hall," I said. "I'll go and see."

I found the bag near the front door. It was made of black leather and looked very, very old. One of its latches was broken, and it was tied up round the middle with a piece of string.

"Thank you," said the Doctor when I brought it to him.

"Was that bag all the luggage you had for your voyage?" I asked.

"Yes," said the Doctor, as he undid the piece of string. "I don't believe in a lot of baggage. It's such a nuisance. Life's too short to fuss with it. And it isn't really necessary, you know — Where *did* I put those sausages?"

The Doctor was feeling about inside the bag. First he brought out a loaf of new bread. Next came a glass jar of marmalade, which he set upon the table. At last the Doctor brought out a pound of sausages.

"Now," he said, "all we want is a frying pan."

We went into the scullery and there we found some pots and pans hanging against the wall. The Doctor took down the frying pan, and in a few moments the sausages were sending a beautiful smell all through the room.

"Ah," said the Doctor. "The sausages are done to a turn. Come along — hold your plate near and let me give you some."

Then we sat down at the kitchen table and started a hearty meal. It was a wonderful kitchen, that. I had many meals there afterward, and I found it a better place to eat in than the grandest dining room in the world. It was so cozy and homelike and warm. It was so handy for the food, too. You took it right off the fire, hot, and put it on the table and ate it. And you could watch your toast toasting at the fender and see it didn't burn while you drank your soup. And if you had forgotten to put the salt on the table, you didn't have to get up and go into another room to fetch it; you just reached round and took the big wooden box off the dresser behind you. Then the fireplace — the biggest fireplace you ever saw — was like a room in itself. You could get right inside it, even when the logs were burning, and sit on the wide seats either side and roast chestnuts after the meal was over — or listen to the kettle singing, or tell stories, or look at picture books by the light of the fire. It was a marvelous kitchen. It was like the Doctor, comfortable, sensible, friendly, and solid.

While we were gobbling away, the door suddenly opened and in marched the duck, Dab-Dab, and the dog, Jip, dragging sheets and pillowcases behind them over the clean tiled floor. The Doctor, seeing how surprised I was, explained:

"They're just going to air the bedding for me in front of the fire. Dab-Dab is a perfect treasure of a housekeeper; she never forgets anything. I had a sister once who used to keep house for me (poor, dear Sarah! I wonder how she's getting on — I haven't seen her in many years). But she wasn't nearly as good as Dab-Dab. Have another sausage?"

The Doctor turned and said a few words to the dog and duck in some strange talk and signs. They seemed to understand him perfectly.

"Can you talk in squirrel language?" I asked.

"Oh yes. That's quite an easy language," said the Doctor. "You could learn that yourself without a great deal of trouble. But why do you ask?"

"Because I have a sick squirrel at home," I said. "I took it away from a hawk. But one of its legs is badly hurt and I wanted very much to have you see it, if you would. Shall I bring it tomorrow?"

"Well, if its leg is badly broken I think I had better see it tonight. It may be too late to do much, but I'll come home with you and take a look at it."

So presently we felt the clothes by the fire, and mine were found to be quite dry. I took them upstairs to the bedroom and changed, and when I came down the Doctor was all ready waiting for me with his little black bag full of medicines and bandages.

"Come along," he said. "The rain has stopped now."

Outside it had grown bright again, and the evening sky was all red with the setting sun; and thrushes were singing in the garden as we opened the gate to go down on to the road.

Polynesia

"IT MUST BE SPLENDID," I said, as we set off in the direction of my home, "to be able to talk all the languages of the different animals. Do you think I could ever learn to do it?"

"Oh, surely," said the Doctor. "With practice. You have to be very patient, you know. You really

42

ought to have Polynesia to start you. It was she who gave me my first lessons."

"Who is Polynesia?" I asked.

"Polynesia was a West African parrot I had. She isn't with me any more now," said the Doctor sadly.

"Why — is she dead?"

"Oh no," said the Doctor. "She is still living, I hope. But when we reached Africa she seemed so glad to get back to her own country. She wept for joy. I left her in Africa — Ah well! I have missed her terribly. She wept again when we left. But I think I did the right thing. She was one of the best friends I ever had. It was she who first gave me the idea of learning the animal languages and becoming an animal doctor. Good old Polynesia! — A most extraordinary bird — Well, well!"

Just at that moment we heard the noise of someone running behind us, and turning around we saw Jip the dog rushing down the road after us as fast as his legs could bring him. He seemed very excited about something, and as soon as he came up to us he started barking and whining to the Doctor in a peculiar way. Then the Doctor too seemed to get all worked up, and began talking and making queer signs to the dog. At length he turned to me, his face shining with happiness.

43

"Polynesia has come back!" he cried. "Imagine it. Jip says she has just arrived at the house. My! And it's five years since I saw her — Excuse me a minute."

He turned as if to go back home. But the parrot, Polynesia, was already flying toward us. The Doctor clapped his hands like a child getting a new toy; while the swarm of sparrows in the roadway fluttered, gossiping, up on to the fences, highly scandalized to see a gray and scarlet parrot skimming down an English lane.

On she came, straight on to the Doctor's shoulder, where she immediately began talking a steady stream in a language I could not understand. She seemed to have a terrible lot to say. And very soon the Doctor had forgotten all about me and my squirrel and Jip and everything else, till at length the bird clearly asked him something about me.

"Oh, excuse me, Stubbins!" said the Doctor. "I was so interested listening to my old friend here. We must get on and see this squirrel of yours — Polynesia, this is Thomas Stubbins."

The parrot, on the Doctor's shoulder, nodded gravely toward me and then, to my great surprise, said quite plainly in English:

"How do you do? I remember the night you were

44

born. It was a terribly cold winter. You were a very ugly baby."

"Stubbins is anxious to learn animal language," said the Doctor. "I was just telling him about you and the lessons you gave me when Jip ran up and told us you had arrived."

"Well," said the parrot, turning to me, "I may have started the Doctor learning, but I never could have done even that if he hadn't first taught me to understand what *I* was saying when I spoke English. You see, many parrots can talk like a person, but very few of them understand what they are saying. They just say it because — well, because they fancy it is smart, or because they know they will get crackers given them."

By this time we had turned and were going toward my home with Jip running in front and Polynesia still perched on the Doctor's shoulder. The bird chattered incessantly, mostly about Africa; but now she spoke in English, out of politeness to me.

"And how is Chee-Chee getting on? — Chee-Chee," added the Doctor in explanation to me, "was a pet monkey I had years ago. I left him in Africa when I came away."

"Well," said Polynesia frowning, "Chee-Chee is

45

not entirely happy. I saw a good deal of him the last few years. He got dreadfully homesick for you and the house and the garden. It's funny, but I was just the same way myself. You remember how crazy I was to get back to the dear old land? And Africa *is* a wonderful country — I don't care what anybody says. Well, I thought I was going to have a perfectly grand time. But somehow — I don't know — after a few weeks it seemed to get tiresome. I just couldn't seem to settle down. Well, to make a long story short, one night I made up my mind that I'd come back here and find you. So I hunted up old Chee-Chee and told him about it. He said he didn't blame me a bit — felt exactly the same way himself.

"When I left, poor old Chee-Chee broke down and cried. He said he felt as though his only friend were leaving him — though, as you know, he has simply millions of relatives there. He said it didn't seem fair that I should have wings to fly over here any time I liked, and him with no way to follow me. But mark my words, I wouldn't be a bit surprised if he found a way to come — someday. He's a smart lad is Chee-Chee."

At this point we arrived at my home. My father's shop was closed and the shutters were up, but my mother was standing at the door looking down the street.

"Good evening, Mrs. Stubbins," said the Doctor. "It is my fault your son is so late. I made him stay to supper while his clothes were drying. He was soaked to the skin, and so was I. We ran into one another in the storm, and I insisted on his coming into my house for shelter."

"I was beginning to get worried about him," said my mother. "I am thankful to you, Sir, for looking after him so well and bringing him home."

"Don't mention it — don't mention it," said the Doctor. "We have had a very interesting chat."

"Who might it be that I have the honor of addressing?" asked my mother, staring at the gray parrot perched on the Doctor's shoulder.

"Oh, I'm John Dolittle. I daresay your husband will remember me. He made me some very excellent boots about four years ago. They really are splendid," added the Doctor, gazing down at his feet with great satisfaction.

"The Doctor has come to cure my squirrel, Mother," said I. "He knows all about animals."

"Oh no," said the Doctor, "not all, Stubbins — not all about them by any means."

"It is very kind of you to come so far to look after

his pet," said my mother. "Tom is always bringing home strange creatures from the woods and the field."

"Is he?" said the Doctor. "Perhaps he will grow up to be a naturalist someday. Who knows?"

Then I led the Doctor to my bedroom at the top of the house and showed him the squirrel in the packing case filled with straw.

The animal, who had always seemed very much afraid of me — though I had tried hard to make him feel at home — sat up at once when the Doctor came into the room and started to chatter. The Doctor chattered back in the same way, and the squirrel, when he was lifted up to have his leg examined, appeared to be rather pleased than frightened.

I held a candle while the Doctor tied the leg up in what he called "splints," which he made out of matchsticks with his penknife.

"I think you will find that his leg will get better now in a very short time," said the Doctor, closing up his bag. "Don't let him run about for at least two weeks yet, but keep him in the open air, and cover him up with dry leaves if the nights get cool. He tells me he is rather lonely here, all by himself, and is wondering how his wife and children are getting on. I have assured him you are a man to be trusted, and I will send a squirrel who lives in my garden to find out how his family are and to bring him news of them. He must be kept cheerful at all costs. Squirrels are naturally a very cheerful, active race. It is very hard for them to lie still doing nothing. But you needn't worry about him. He will be all right."

After we had seen the Doctor out at the front door, we all came back into the parlor and talked about him till midnight.

My Education Begins

MANY WEEKS LATER, with the help of Polynesia, I began to learn the animals' languages. Oh, I was slow at first, and Polynesia often scolded me for not remembering something that she had told me over and over. But gradually I could interpret all the wigglings of tails and twitching of noses and squeaks and squawks that formed the animals' messages to humans.

When I thought I was ready, I asked Polynesia to speak to the Doctor on my behalf.

"You mean you want to be a proper assistant to the Doctor, is that it?" she asked.

"Yes, I suppose that's what you call it," I answered. "You know you said yourself that you thought I could be very useful to him."

"Humph — Let's go and speak to the Doctor about it," said Polynesia. "He's in the next room — in the study. Open the door very gently — he may be working and not want to be disturbed."

Presently the Doctor looked up and saw us at the door.

"Oh — come in, Stubbins," said he. "Did you wish to speak to me? Come in and take a chair."

"Doctor," I said, "I want to be a naturalist — like you — when I grow up."

"Oh you do, do you?" murmured the Doctor. "Humph — Well! — Dear me! — You don't say! — Well, well! Have you, er — have you spoken to your mother and father about it?"

"No, not yet," I said. "I want you to speak to them for me. You would do it better. I want to be your helper — your assistant — if you'll have me."

"What arrangement was it that you thought of?" asked the Doctor.

"Well, I thought," said I, "that perhaps you would come and see my mother and father and tell them that if they let me live here with you and work hard, that you will teach me to read and write. You see my mother is awfully anxious to have me learn reading and writing. And besides, I couldn't be a proper naturalist without, could I?"

"Oh, I don't know so much about that," said the Doctor. "It is nice, I admit, to be able to read and write. But naturalists are not all alike, you know. For example, this young fellow Charles Darwin that people are talking about so much now — he's a Cambridge graduate — reads and writes very well. And then Cuvier — he used to be a tutor. But listen, the greatest naturalist of them all doesn't even know how to write his own name nor to read the ABC."

"Who is he?" I asked.

"He is a mysterious person," said the Doctor — "a very mysterious person. His name is Long Arrow, the son of Golden Arrow. He is a Red Indian."

"Have you ever seen him?" I asked.

"No," said the Doctor, "I've never seen him. No white man has ever met him. I fancy Mr. Darwin doesn't even know that he exists. He lives almost entirely with the animals and with the different tribes of Indians — usually somewhere among the mountains of Peru. Never stays long in one place. Goes from tribe to tribe, like a sort of Indian tramp."

"How do you know so much about him," I asked, "if you've never even seen him?"

"The Purple Bird of Paradise," said the Doctor — "she told me all about him. She says he is a perfectly marvelous naturalist. I got her to take a message to him for me last time she was here. I am expecting her back any day now. I can hardly wait to see what answer she has brought from him. It is already almost the last week of August. I do hope nothing has happened to her on the way."

"But why do the animals and birds come to you when they are sick?" I said. "Why don't they go to him, if he is so very wonderful?"

"It seems that my methods are more up to date," said the Doctor. "But from what the Purple Bird of Paradise tells me, Long Arrow's knowledge of natural history must be positively tremendous. His specialty is botany — plants and all that sort of thing. But he knows a lot about birds and animals, too. He's very good on bees and beetles — But now tell me, Stubbins, are you quite sure that you really want to be a naturalist?"

"Yes," said I, "my mind is made up."

"Well you know, it isn't a very good profession for making money. Not at all, it isn't. Most of the good naturalists don't make any money whatever. All they do is spend money buying butterfly nets and cases for birds' eggs and things. It is only now, after I have been a naturalist for many years, that I am beginning to make a little money from the books I write."

"I don't care about money," I said. "I want to be a naturalist." I hesitated a minute before I went on. "You see, there's another thing: if I'm living with you, and sort of belong to your house and business, I shall be able to come with you next time you go on a voyage."

"Oh, I see," said he, smiling. "So you want to come on a voyage with me, do you? — Ah hah!"

"I want to go on all your voyages with you. It would be much easier for you if you had someone to carry the butterfly nets and notebooks. Wouldn't it now?"

For a long time the Doctor sat thinking, drumming on the desk with his fingers, while I waited, terribly impatiently, to see what he was going to say.

At last he shrugged his shoulders and stood up.

"Well, Stubbins," said he, "I'll come and talk it over with you and your parents — say — next Thursday. And — well, we'll see. We'll see."

Then I tore home like the wind to tell my mother and father that the Doctor was coming to see them next Thursday.

The next day I was sitting on the wall of the Doctor's garden after tea, talking to Dab-Dab. Over in one corner of the garden a small sparrow was standing on the sundial, swearing at some blackbird down below.

"Who is that?" I asked Dab-Dab.

"Oh, that is Cheapside!" she replied, ruffling her feathers. "He's a cheeky, rude, London sparrow who lives around St. Paul's Cathedral. But the Doctor likes him — " She shrugged her wings. "We put up with him because of that!"

Suddenly I heard a curious distant noise down the road, toward the town. It sounded like a lot of people cheering. I stood up on the wall to see if I could make out what was coming. Presently there appeared round a bend a great crowd of schoolchildren following a very ragged, curious-looking woman.

"What in the world can it be?" cried Dab-Dab.

The children were all laughing and shouting. And certainly the woman they were following was most extraordinary. She had very long arms and the most stooping shoulders I have ever seen. She wore a straw hat on the side of her head with poppies on it, and her skirt was so long for her it dragged on the ground like a ball-gown's train. I could not see anything of her face because of the wide hat pulled over her eyes. But as she got nearer to us and the laughing of the children grew louder, I noticed that her hands were very dark in color, and hairy, like a witch's.

Then all of a sudden Dab-Dab at my side startled me by crying out in a loud voice:

"Why it's Chee-Chee! — Chee-Chee come back at last! How dare those children tease him! I'll give the little imps something to laugh at!"

And she flew right off the wall down into the road and made straight for the children, squawking away in a most terrifying fashion and pecking at their feet and legs. The children made off down the street back to the town as hard as they could run.

The strange-looking figure in the straw hat stood gazing after them a moment and then came wearily up to the gate. It didn't bother to undo the latch, but just climbed right over the gate as though it were something in the way. And then I noticed that it took hold of the bars with its feet, so that it really had four hands to climb with. But it was only when I at last got a glimpse of the face under the hat that I could be really sure it was a monkey.

Chee-Chee — for it was he — frowned at me suspiciously from the top of the gate, as though he thought I was going to laugh at him like the other boys and girls. Then he dropped into the garden on the inside and immediately started taking off his clothes. He tore the straw hat in two and threw it down into the road. Then he took off his bodice and skirt, and jumped on them savagely and began kicking them round the front garden.

Presently I heard a screech from the house, and out flew Polynesia, followed by the Doctor and Jip.

"Chee-Chee! — Chee-Chee!" shouted the parrot. "You've come at last! I always told the Doctor you'd find a way. How ever did you do it?"

They all gathered round him, shaking him by his

four hands, laughing, and asking him a million questions at once. Then they all started back for the house.

"Run up to my bedroom, Stubbins," said the Doctor, turning to me. "You'll find a bag of peanuts in the small left-hand drawer of the bureau. I have always kept them there in case he might come back unexpectedly someday. And wait a minute — see if Dab-Dab has any bananas in the pantry. Chee-Chee hasn't had a banana, he tells me, in two months."

When I came down again to the kitchen I found everybody listening attentively to the monkey, who was telling the story of his journey from Africa.

The Purple Bird
of Paradise

THE NEXT THURSDAY, the doctor came to my
house. The result was that my parents agreed
to let me live and study with Doctor Dolittle.

One day, as we were returning to the house, we

found Polynesia waiting for us on the front porch. She looked full of important news.

"Doctor," said she, "the Purple Bird of Paradise has arrived!"

"At last!" said the Doctor. "I had begun to fear some accident had befallen her. And how is Miranda?"

"Oh, she seemed all right when she arrived," said Polynesia — "but the mischief-making sparrow, Cheapside, insulted her as soon as she came into the garden. She's in the study now. And I shut Cheapside in one of your bookcases — you can deal with *him!*"

In the center of the study-room table, perched on the inkstand, stood the most beautiful bird I have ever seen. She had a deep violet-colored breast, scarlet wings, and a long, long sweeping tail of gold. Already she had her head tucked under her wing.

"Sh!" said Dab-Dab. "Miranda is asleep."

The noisy little sparrow was fluttering angrily against the glass of the bookcase.

"Let Cheapside out, please," whispered the Doctor.

Dab-Dab opened the bookcase door and the

sparrow strutted out, trying hard not to look guilty.

"Cheapside," said the Doctor sternly, "what did you say to Miranda?"

"I didn't say nothin', Doc, straight I didn't. That is, nothin' much. She comes swankin' into the garden, turnin' up 'er nose in all directions. And all I said was, 'You don't belong in an English garden; you ought to be in a milliner's shop.' That's all!"

"You should be ashamed of yourself, Cheapside," said the Doctor. "Leave the room!"

Sheepishly, but still trying to look as though he didn't care, Cheapside hopped out into the passage and Dab-Dab closed the door.

The Doctor went up to the beautiful bird on the inkstand and gently stroked its back. Instantly its head popped out from under its wing.

"Well, Miranda," said the Doctor, "I'm terribly sorry this has happened. But you mustn't mind Cheapside; he doesn't know any better. He's a city bird, and all his life he has had to squabble for a living. You must make allowances."

Miranda stretched her gorgeous wings wearily. Now that I saw her awake and moving, I noticed what a superior, well-bred manner she had. There were tears in her eyes, and her beak was trembling.

"I wouldn't have minded so much," she said in a high silvery voice, "if I hadn't been so dreadfully worn out — that and something else," she added beneath her breath.

"Did you have a hard time getting here?" asked the Doctor.

"The worst passage I ever made," said Miranda. "The weather — well there. What's the use? I'm here anyway."

"Tell me," said the Doctor as though he had been impatiently waiting to say something for a long time, "what did Long Arrow say when you gave him my message?"

The Purple Bird of Paradise hung her head.

"That's the worst part of it," she said. "I might almost as well have not come at all. I wasn't able to deliver your message. I couldn't find him. *Long Arrow, the son of Golden Arrow, has disappeared!*"

"Disappeared!" cried the Doctor. "Why, what's become of him?"

"Nobody knows," Miranda answered. "He had often disappeared before, as I have told you — so that the Indians didn't know where he was. But it's a mighty hard thing to hide away from the birds. I had always been able to find some owl or martin who could tell me where he was, if I wanted to know. But not this time. That's why I'm nearly a fortnight late in coming to you. I kept hunting and hunting, asking everywhere. I went over the whole length and breadth of South America, but there wasn't a living thing could tell me where he was."

There was a sad silence in the room after she had finished. The Doctor was frowning in a peculiar sort of way, and Polynesia scratched her head.

"Did you ask the black parrots?" asked Polynesia. "They usually know everything."

"Certainly I did," said Miranda. "And I was so upset at not being able to find out anything that I forgot all about observing the weather signs before I started my flight here. I didn't even bother to break my journey at the Azores, but cut right across, making for the Straits of Gibraltar — as though it were June or July. And of course I ran into a perfectly frightful storm in mid-Atlantic. I really thought I'd never come through it. Luckily I found a piece of a wrecked vessel floating in the sea after the storm had partly died down, and I roosted on it and took some sleep. If I hadn't been able to take that rest I wouldn't be here to tell the tale."

"Poor Miranda. What a time you must have had!" said the Doctor. "But tell me, were you able to find out whereabouts Long Arrow was last seen?"

"Yes. A young albatross told me he had seen him on Spidermonkey Island."

"Spidermonkey Island? That's somewhere off the coast of Brazil, isn't it?"

"Yes, that's it. Of course I flew there right away and asked every bird on the island — and it is a big island, a hundred miles long. I nearly got caught and put in a cage for my pains, too. That's the worst of having beautiful feathers — it's as much as your life is worth to go near most humans. They say, 'Oh, how pretty!' and shoot an arrow or bullet into you. You and Long Arrow were the only men that I would ever trust myself near — out of all the people in the world."

"But you don't really think that he is dead, do you?" asked the Doctor.

"What else can I think," asked Miranda, bursting into tears, "when for six whole months he has not been seen by flesh, fish, or fowl?"

Blind Travel

THIS NEWS ABOUT LONG ARROW made us all very sad. And I could see from the silent dreamy way the Doctor took his tea that he was dreadfully upset.

I did my best to cheer him up by reminding him about our plans for a voyage.

"But you see, Stubbins," said he as we rose from the table and Dab-Dab and Chee-Chee began to clear away, "I don't know where to go now. I feel sort of lost since Miranda brought me this news. On this voyage I had planned going to see Long Arrow. I had been looking forward to it for a whole year. I felt he might help me in learning the language of the shellfish, and perhaps in finding some way of getting to the bottom of the sea. But now he's gone! And all his great knowledge has gone with him."

Then he seemed to fall adreaming again.

We went back into the study, where Jip brought the Doctor his slippers and his pipe. And after the pipe was lit and the smoke began to fill the room, the old man seemed to cheer up a little,

"But you will go on some voyage, Doctor, won't you," I asked — "even if you can't go to find Long Arrow?"

He looked up sharply into my face, and I suppose he saw how anxious I was. Because he suddenly smiled his old boyish smile and said, "Yes, Stubbins. Don't worry. We'll go. We mustn't stop working and learning, even if poor Long Arrow has disappeared. But where to go? — that's the question. Where shall we go?"

66

There were so many places that I wanted to go that I couldn't make up my mind right away. And while I was still thinking, the Doctor said, "I'll tell you what we'll do, Stubbins — it's a game I used to play when I was young, before Sarah came to live with me. I used to call it Blind Travel. Whenever I wanted to go on a voyage, and couldn't make up my mind where to go, I would take the atlas and open it with my eyes shut. Next, I'd wave a pencil, still without looking, and stick it down on whatever page had fallen open. Then I'd open my eyes and look. It's a very exciting game, is Blind Travel. Because you have to swear, before you begin, that you will go to the place the pencil touches, come what may. Shall we play it?"

"Oh, let's!" I almost yelled. "How thrilling! I hope it's China — or Borneo — or Bagdad."

And in a moment I had scrambled up the bookcase, dragged the big atlas from the top shelf, and laid it on the table before the Doctor.

I knew every page in that atlas by heart. How many days and nights I had lingered over its old faded maps, following the blue rivers from the mountains to the sea, wondering what the little towns really looked like and how wide were the sprawling lakes! I had had a lot of fun with that atlas, traveling, in my mind, all over the world.

As the Doctor began sharpening his pencil, a thought came to me.

"What if the pencil falls upon the North Pole?" I asked. "Will we have to go there?"

"No. The rules of the game say you don't have to go any place you've been before. You are allowed another try. I've been to the North Pole," he ended quietly, "so we shan't have to go there."

I could hardly speak with astonishment.

"You've been to the North Pole!" I managed to gasp out at last. "But I thought it was still undiscovered. The map shows all the places explorers have reached to, *trying* to get there. Why isn't your name down if you discovered it?"

"I promised to keep it a secret. And you must promise me never to tell any one. Yes, I discovered the North Pole in April, 1809. But shortly after I got there, the polar bears came to me in a body and told me there was a great deal of coal there, buried beneath the snow. They knew, they said, that human beings would do anything, and go anywhere, to get coal. So would I please keep it a secret. Because once people began coming up there to start coal mines, their beautiful white country would be spoiled — and there was nowhere else in the world cold enough for polar bears to be comfortable. So of course I had to promise them I would. Well now, are we ready? — Good! Take the pencil and stand here close to the table. When the book falls open, wave the pencil round three times and jab it down. Ready? — All right. Shut your eyes."

It was a tense and fearful moment, but very thrilling. We both had our eyes shut tight. I heard the atlas fall open with a bang. I wondered what page it was, England or Asia. If it should be the map of Asia, so much would depend on where that pencil would land. I waved three times in a circle. I began to lower my hand. The pencil point touched the page.

"All right," I called out, "it's done!"

We both opened our eyes, then bumped our heads together with a crack in our eagerness to lean over and see where we were to go.

The atlas lay open at a map called, "Chart of the South Atlantic Ocean." My pencil point was resting right in the center of a tiny island. The name of it was printed so small that the Doctor had to get out his strong spectacles to read it. I was trembling with excitement.

"Spidermonkey Island," he read out slowly.

Then he whistled softly beneath his breath. "Of all the extraordinary things. You've hit upon the very island where Long Arrow was last seen on earth. I wonder — Well, well! How very singular! — Well, there's one good thing about it: I shall be able to get some Jabizri beetles."

"What are Jabizri beetles?"

"They are a very rare kind of beetle with peculiar habits. I want to study them. There are only three countries in the world where they are to be found. Spidermonkey Island is one of them. But even there they are very scarce."

"What is this little question mark after the name of the island for?" I asked, pointing to the map.

"That means that the island's position in the ocean is not known very exactly — that it is somewhere *about* there."

At this point the poor Bird of Paradise stirred and woke up. In our excitement we had forgotten to speak low.

"We are going to Spidermonkey Island, Miranda," said the Doctor. "You know where it is, do you not?"

"I know where it was the last time I saw it," said the bird. "But whether it will be there still, I can't say."

"What do you mean?" asked the Doctor. "It is always in the same place surely?"

"Not by any means," said Miranda. "Why, didn't you know? — Spidermonkey Island is a *floating* island. It moves all over the place — usually somewhere near southern South America. But of course I could find it for you if you want to go there."

At this fresh piece of news I could contain myself no longer. I was bursting to tell someone. I ran dancing and singing from the room to find Chee-Chee.

At the door I tripped over Dab-Dab, who was just coming in with her wings full of plates, and fell headlong on my nose.

"Has the boy gone crazy?" cried the duck. "Where do you think you're going, ninny?"

"To Spidermonkey Island!" I shouted, picking myself up and doing cart wheels down the hall — "Spidermonkey Island! Hooray! — And it's a *floating* island!"

"You're going to Bedlam, I should say," snorted the housekeeper. "Look what you've done to my best china!"

But I was far too happy to listen to her scolding, and I ran on, singing, into the kitchen to find Chee-Chee.

Bad Weather

DOCTOR DOLITTLE was able to buy the neatest, prettiest vessel that ever was built. It was named the *Curlew*. We sailed to Spidermonkey Island with a crew of three: Doctor Dolittle, myself, and Matthew Mugg, the Cat's Meat Man. Chee-Chee, Jip, and Polynesia were the only animals to go with us.

One day after we had been at sea for many weeks, I noticed something peculiar. We were not going as fast as we had been. Our favorable wind had almost entirely disappeared. The *Curlew* just dawdled along at the speed of a toddling babe.

I now saw that the Doctor was becoming uneasy. He kept getting out his sextant (an instrument which tells you what part of the ocean you are in) and making calculations.

"But, Doctor," I said, when I found him one afternoon mumbling to himself about the misty appearance of the sky, "it wouldn't matter so much, would it, if we did take a little longer over the trip? We've got plenty to eat on board, and the Purple Bird of Paradise will know that we have been delayed by something that we couldn't help."

"Yes, I suppose so," he said thoughtfully. "But I hate to keep her waiting. At this season of the year she generally goes to the Peruvian mountains — for her health. Ah, here comes a wind — not very strong — but maybe it'll grow."

A gentle breeze from the northeast came singing through the ropes, and we smiled up hopefully at the *Curlew*'s leaning masts.

"We've only got another hundred and fifty

73

miles to make, to sight the coast of Brazil," said the Doctor. "If that wind would just stay with us steady for a full day, we'd see land."

But suddenly the wind changed, swung to the east, then back to the northeast, then to the north. It came in fitful gusts, as though it hadn't made up its mind which way to blow; and I was kept busy at the wheel, swinging the *Curlew* this way and that to keep the right side of it.

Presently we heard Polynesia, who was in the rigging keeping a lookout for land or passing ships, screech down to us:

"Bad weather coming. That jumpy wind is an ugly sign. And look! — over there in the east — see that black line, low down? If that isn't a storm, I'm a landlubber. The gales round here are fierce when they do blow — tear your canvas out like paper. You take the wheel, Doctor: it'll need strong arms if it's a real storm. I'll go wake Jip and Chee-Chee. This looks bad to me. We'd best get all the sail down right away, till we see how strong she's going to blow."

I must confess I was frightened. You see, so far I had only seen the sea in friendly moods — sometimes quiet and lazy; sometimes laughing, venturesome, and reckless; sometimes brooding and poetic, when moonbeams turn her ripples into silver threads and dreaming snowy night clouds piled up fairy castles in the sky. But as yet I had not known, or even guessed at, the terrible strength of the sea's wild anger.

When that storm finally struck us, we leaned right over flatly on our side, as though some invisible giant had slapped the poor *Curlew* on the cheek.

After that things happened so thick and so fast that, what with the wind that stopped your breath, the driving, blinding water, the deafening noise, and the rest, I haven't a very clear idea of how our shipwreck came about.

I remember seeing the sails, which we were now trying to roll up upon the deck, torn out of our hands by the wind and go overboard like a penny balloon — very nearly carrying Chee-Chee with them. And I have a dim recollection of Polynesia screeching somewhere for one of us to go downstairs and close the portholes.

In spite of our masts being bare of sail we were now scudding along to the southward at a great pace. But every once in a while huge gray-black waves would arise from under the ship's side like nightmare monsters, swell and climb, then crash down upon us, pressing us into the sea; and the poor *Curlew* would come to a standstill, half under water, like a gasping, drowning pig.

While I was clambering along toward the wheel to see the Doctor, clinging like a leech with hands and legs to the rails lest I be blown overboard, one of these tremendous seas tore loose my hold, filled my throat with water, and swept me like a cork the full length of the deck. My head struck a door with an awful bang. And then I fainted.

When I awoke, I was very hazy in my head. The sky was blue and the sea was calm. At first I thought I must have fallen asleep in the sun on the deck of the *Curlew*. And thinking that I would be late for my turn at the wheel, I tried to rise to my feet. I found I couldn't; my arms were tied to something behind me with a piece of rope. By twisting my neck around I found this to be a mast, broken off short. Then I realized that I wasn't sitting on a ship at all, I was only sitting on a piece of one. I began to feel uncomfortably scared. Screwing up my eyes, I searched the rim of the sea north, east, south, and west: no land, no ships; nothing was in sight. I was alone in the ocean!

At last, little by little, my bruised head hurt less and I began to remember what had happened. Working my hand into my pocket, I found my pen-knife and cut the rope that tied me. This reminded me of a shipwreck story which Joe had once told me, of a captain who had tied his son to a mast in order that he shouldn't be washed overboard by the gale. So of course it must have been the Doctor who had done the same to me.

But where was he? And where were the others?

The awful thought came to me that the Doctor and the rest of them must be drowned, since there was no other wreckage to be seen upon the waters. I got to my feet and stared around the sea again. Nothing — nothing but water and sky!

Presently, a long way off, I saw the small dark shape of a bird skimming low down over the swell. When it came quite close, I saw it was a stormy petrel. Twice it circled round my raft, lazily, with hardly a flip of the wing. And then it went off in the direction from which it had come. And I was alone once more.

I found I was somewhat hungry, and a little thirsty too. I began to think all sorts of miserable thoughts, the way one does when one is lonesome and has missed breakfast. What was going to become of me now, if the Doctor and the rest were drowned? I would starve to death or die of thirst.

I went on like this for a while, growing gloomier and gloomier, when suddenly I thought of Polynesia. "You're always safe with the Doctor," she had said. "He gets there. Remember that."

I'm sure I wouldn't have minded so much if he had been here with me. It was this being all alone that made me uneasy. But if what Polynesia had said was true, he couldn't be drowned, and things would come out all right in the end somehow.

I threw out my chest, buttoned up my collar, and began walking up and down the short raft to keep warm. I would be like John Dolittle. I wouldn't cry — and I wouldn't get excited.

How long I paced back and forth I don't know. But it was a long time, for I had nothing else to do.

At last I got tired and lay down to rest. And in spite of all my troubles, I soon fell fast asleep.

"Are you awake?" said a high silvery voice at my elbow.

I sprang up as though someone had stuck a pin in me. And there, perched at the very end of my raft, her beautiful golden tail glowing dimly in the starlight, sat Miranda, the Purple Bird of Paradise!

Never have I been so glad to see anyone in my life. I almost fell into the water as I leapt to hug her.

"I didn't want to wake you," said she. "I guessed you must be tired after all you've been through — Don't squash the life out of me, boy; I'm not a stuffed duck, you know."

"Oh, Miranda, you dear old thing," said I, "I'm so glad to see you. Tell me, where is the Doctor? Is he alive?"

"Of course he's alive, and it's my firm belief he always will be. He's over there, about forty miles to the westward."

"What's he doing there?"

"He's sitting on the other half of the *Curlew* shaving himself — or he was, when I left him."

"Well, thank heaven he's alive!" said I — "And the animals, are they all right?"

"Yes, they're with him. Your ship broke in half in the storm. The Doctor had tied you down when he found you stunned. And the part you were on got separated and floated away. Golly, it *was* a storm! It was the petrel that first gave us the tip where you were."

"Well, but how can I get to the Doctor, Miranda? — I haven't any oars."

"Get to him! — Why, you're going to him now. Look behind you."

I turned around. The moon was just rising on the sea's edge. And I now saw that my raft was moving through the water, but so gently that I had not noticed it before.

"What's moving us?" I asked.

"Some porpoises," said Miranda.

I went to the back of the raft and looked down into the water. And just below the surface I could see the dim forms of four big porpoises, their sleek skins glinting in the moonlight, pushing at the raft with their noses.

"They're old friends of the Doctor's," said Miranda. "They'd do anything for John Dolittle."

Presently, from somewhere in the murky dusk, I heard Polynesia singing a sailor's song — just as though she were back at Puddleby in the warm kitchen by the fireside. And in a little, by peering and peering in the direction of the sound, I at last made out a dim mass of tattered, splintered wreckage — all that remained of the poor *Curlew* — floating low down upon the water.

A hulloa came through the night. And I answered it. We kept it up, calling to one another back and forth across the calm night sea. And a few minutes later the two halves of our brave little ruined ship bumped gently together again.

Close down to the edge of the water, using the sea's calm surface for a mirror and a piece of broken bottle for a razor, John Dolittle was shaving his face by the light of the moon.

Land!

THEY ALL GAVE ME A GREAT GREETING as I clambered off my half of the ship onto theirs. The Doctor brought me a wonderful drink of fresh water, which he drew from a barrel, and Chee-Chee and Polynesia stood around me feeding me ship's biscuit.

But it was the sight of the Doctor's smiling face — just knowing that I was with him once again — that cheered me more than anything else. Just to be with him gave you a wonderful feeling of comfort and safety.

Except for his appearance (his clothes were crumpled and damp, and his battered high hat was stained with salt water), that storm which had so terrified me had disturbed him no more than bumping into me on the Oxenthorpe Road that rainy night months ago.

Politely thanking Miranda for getting me so quickly, he asked her if she would now go ahead of us and show us the way to Spidermonkey Island. Next, he gave orders to the porpoises to leave my old piece of the ship and push the bigger half wherever the Bird of Paradise should lead us.

How much he had lost in the wreck besides his razor, I did not know — everything, most likely, together with all the money he owned. And still he was smiling as though he wanted for nothing in the world. The only things he had saved, as far as I could see — beyond the barrel of water and bag of biscuit — were his precious notebooks. These, I saw when he stood up, he had strapped around his waist with yards and yards of twine.

The only inconvenience we suffered from was the cold. This seemed to increase as we went forward. The Doctor said that the island, disturbed from its usual paths by the great gale, had evidently drifted farther south than it had ever been before.

On the third night, poor Miranda came back to us nearly frozen. She told the Doctor that in the morning we would find the island quite close to us, though we couldn't see it now as it was a misty dark night. She said that she must hurry back at once to a warmer climate, and that she would visit the Doctor in Puddleby next August as usual.

After the Doctor had thanked her again and again for all that she had done for us, she wished us good luck and disappeared into the night.

We were all awake early in the morning, long before it was light, waiting for our first glimpse of the country we had come so far to see. And as the rising sun turned the eastern sky to gray, of course it was old Polynesia who first shouted that she could see palm trees and mountaintops.

The porpoises gave us one last push, and our strange-looking craft bumped gently on a low beach. Then, thanking our lucky stars for a chance to stretch our cramped legs, we all bundled off on to the land — the first land, even though it was floating land, that we had trodden for six weeks. What a thrill I felt as I realized that Spidermonkey Island, the little spot in the atlas which my pencil had touched, lay at last beneath my feet!

When the light increased still further we noticed that the palms and grasses of the island seemed withered and almost dead. The Doctor said that it must be on account of the cold that the island was now suffering from in its new climate. These trees and grasses, he told us, were the kind that belonged to warm, tropical weather.

As we were preparing to go inland and explore the island, we suddenly noticed a whole band of Red Indians watching us with great curiosity from among the trees. The Doctor went forward to talk to them. He tried by signs to show them that he had come on a friendly visit. The Indians didn't seem to like us, however. They evidently wanted us to leave the island at once. It was a very uncomfortable situation.

At last the Doctor made them understand that he only wanted to see the island all over, and that then he would go away — though how he meant to do it, with no boat to sail in, was more than I could imagine.

While they were talking among themselves, another Indian arrived — apparently with a message that they were wanted in some other part of the island. Because presently, shaking their spears threateningly at us, they went off with the newcomer.

"They're going off to their village," said Polynesia. "I'll bet there's a village on the other side of those mountains. If you take my advice, Doctor, you'll get away from this beach while their backs are turned. They may grow friendlier when they see we mean no harm. They have honest, open faces and look like a decent crowd to me. They're just ignorant — probably never saw white folks before."

So, feeling a little bit discouraged by our first reception, we moved off toward the mountains in the center of the island.

Polynesia and Chee-Chee were good guides and splendid jungle hunters, and the two of them set to work at once looking for food for us. In a very short space of time they had found quite a number of different fruits and nuts, which made excellent eating, though none of us knew the names of any of them. We discovered a nice clean stream of good water which came down from the mountains, so we were supplied with something to drink as well.

We followed the stream up toward the heights. And presently we came to parts where the woods were thinner and the ground rocky and steep. Here we could get glimpses of wonderful views all over the island, with the blue sea beyond.

While we were admiring one of these, the Doctor suddenly said, "Sh! — A Jabizri! — Don't you hear it?"

We listened and heard, somewhere in the air about us, an extraordinary musical hum — like a bee, but not just one note. This hum rose and fell, up and down — almost like someone singing.

"No other insect but the Jabizri beetle hums like that," said the Doctor. "I wonder where he is — quite near, by the sound — flying among the trees probably. Oh look! There he goes!"

A huge beetle — easily three inches long, I should say — suddenly flew by our noses. The Doctor got frightfully excited. He took off his hat to use as a net, swooped at the beetle, and caught it. From his pocket he brought out a glass-topped box, and into this he very skillfully made the beetle walk from under the rim of the hat. Then he rose up happy as a child, to examine his new treasure through the glass lid.

It certainly was a most beautiful insect. It was pale blue underneath, but its back was glossy black with huge red spots on it.

"There isn't an entymologist in the whole world who wouldn't give all he has to be in my shoes today," said the Doctor — "Hulloa! This Jabizri's got something on his leg — Doesn't look like mud. I wonder what it is."

He took the beetle carefully out of the box and held it by its back in his fingers, where it waved its six legs slowly in the air. We all crowded about him, peering at it. Rolled around the middle section of its right foreleg was something that looked like a thin dried leaf. It was bound on very neatly with strong spider web.

It was marvelous to see how John Dolittle, with his fat heavy fingers, undid that cobweb cord and unrolled the leaf whole, without tearing it or hurting the precious beetle. The Jabizri he put back into the box. Then he spread the leaf out flat and examined it.

For several moments there was a dead silence while we all stared at the leaf, fascinated and mystified.

"I think this is written in blood," said the Doctor at last. "It turns that color when it's dry. Somebody pricked his finger to make these pictures. It's an old dodge when you're short of ink, but highly unsanitary. What an extraordinary thing to find tied to a beetle's leg! I wish I could talk beetle language and find out where the Jabizri got it from."

"But what is it?" I asked — "Rows of little pictures and signs. What do you make of it, Doctor?"

"It's a letter," he said — "a picture letter."

Then he fell to muttering over the pictures.

All of a sudden the Doctor looked up sharply at me, a wonderful smile of delighted understanding spreading over his face.

"*Long Arrow!*" he cried. "Don't you see, Stubbins? — Why, of course! Only a naturalist would think of doing a thing like this: giving his letter to a beetle — not to a common beetle, but to the rarest of all, one that other naturalists would try to catch — Well, well! Long Arrow! — A picture letter from Long Arrow. For pictures are the only writing that he knows."

"Yes, but who is the letter to?" I asked.

"It's to me very likely. Miranda had told him, I know, years ago, that someday I meant to come here. But if not for me, then it's for any one who caught the beetle and read it. It's a letter to the world."

"Well, but what does it say? It doesn't seem to me that it's much good to you now you've got it."

"Yes, it is," he said, "because, look, I can read it now. First picture: men walking up a mountain — that's Long Arrow and his party; men going into a hole in a mountain — they enter a cave looking for medicine plants or mosses; a mountain falling down — some hanging rocks must have slipped and trapped them, imprisoned them in the cave. And this was the only living creature that could carry a message for them to the outside world — a beetle, who could burrow his way into the open air. Now look at the next picture: men pointing to their open mouths — they are hungry; men pray-ing — begging anyone who finds this letter to come to their assistance; men lying down — they are sick, or starving. This letter, Stubbins, is their last cry for help."

He sprang to his feet as he ended, snatched out a

notebook, and put the letter between the leaves. His hands were trembling with haste and agitation.

"Come on!" he cried. "Up the mountain, all of you. There's not a moment to lose. Stubbins, bring the water and nuts with you. Heaven only knows how long they've been pining underground. Let's hope and pray we're not too late!"

"But where are you going to look?" I asked.

"Didn't you see from the picture?" he said, grabbing up his hat from the ground and cramming it on his head. "It was an oddly shaped mountain — looked like a hawk's head. Well, there's where he is — if he's still alive. First thing for us to do is to get up on a high peak and look around the island for a mountain shaped like a hawk's head. Come on! Hurry! To delay may mean death to the greatest naturalist ever born!"

Hawk's Head Mountain

WHEN WE HAD SCRAMBLED TO THE TOP of a high peak, almost instantly we saw the strange mountain pictured in the letter. In shape, it was the perfect image of a hawk's head, and was, as far as we could see, the second highest summit in the island.

With one look at the sun for direction, down the Doctor dashed again, taking all the short cuts. For a fat man, he was certainly the swiftest cross-country runner I ever saw.

I floundered after him as fast as I could. Jip, Chee-Chee, and Polynesia were a long way ahead — even beyond the Doctor — enjoying the hunt like a paper chase.

When we reached the foot of the mountain, the Doctor said,

"Now we will separate and search for caves. If anyone finds anything like a cave or a hole where the earth and rocks have fallen in, he must shout and hulloa to the rest of us. If we find nothing, we will all gather here in about an hour's time. Everybody understand?"

Then we all went off on our different ways.

Each of us, you may be sure, was anxious to be the one to make a discovery. And never was a mountain searched so thoroughly. But alas! nothing could we find that looked in the least like a fallen-in cave.

One by one, tired and disappointed, we straggled back to the meeting place. The Doctor seemed gloomy and impatient, but by no means inclined to give up.

"Polynesia," asked the Doctor, "did you see *nothing* that might put us on the right track?"

"Not a thing, Doctor — But I have a plan."

"Oh, good!" cried John Dolittle, full of hope renewed. "What is it? Let's hear it."

"You still have that beetle with you," she asked — "the Biz-biz, or whatever it is you call the wretched insect?"

"Yes," said the Doctor, producing the glass-topped box from his pocket, "here it is."

"All right. Now listen," said she. "If what you have supposed is true — that is, that Long Arrow had been trapped inside the mountain by falling rock, he probably found that beetle inside the cave — perhaps many other different beetles too, eh? He wouldn't have been likely to take the Biz-biz in with him, would he? — He was hunting plants, you say, not beetles. Isn't that right?"

"Yes," said the Doctor, "that's probably so."

"All right. Then the thing to do is to let the beetle go — and watch him; and sooner or later he'll return to his home in Long Arrow's cave. And there we will follow him. Or at all events," she added, smoothing down her wing feathers with a very superior air, "we will follow him till the miserable bug starts nosing under the earth. But at least he will show us what part of the mountain Long Arrow is hidden in."

"But he may fly, if I let him out," said the Doctor. "Then we shall just lose him and be no better off than we were before."

"*Let* him fly," snorted Polynesia scornfully. "A parrot can wing it as fast as a Biz-biz, I fancy. If he takes to the air, I'll guarantee not to let the little devil out of my sight."

"Splendid!" cried the Doctor. "Polynesia, you have a great brain. I'll set him to work at once and see what happens."

Again we all clustered round the Doctor as he carefully lifted off the glass lid and let the big beetle climb out upon his finger.

"Doctor," said Polynesia, "why not tie another message to the creature's leg, telling Long Arrow that we're doing our best to reach him and that he mustn't give up hope?"

"I will," said the Doctor. And in a minute he had pulled a dry leaf from a bush nearby and was covering it with little pictures in pencil.

At last, neatly fixed up with his new mailbag, Mr. Jabizri crawled off the Doctor's finger to the ground and looked about him. He stretched his legs, polished his nose with his front feet, and then moved off leisurely to the westward.

We had expected him to walk *up* the mountain; instead, he walked *around* it. Do you know how long it takes a beetle to walk round a mountain? Well, I assure you it takes an unbelievably long time. As the hours dragged by, we hoped and hoped that he would get up and fly the rest, and let Polynesia carry on the work of following him. But he never opened his wings once.

After he had led us the whole way round the mountain, he brought us to the exact spot where we started from, and there he came to a dead stop.

"Well," said Polynesia, "a lot of good that trip was. He doesn't even have enough sense to go home."

"Maybe he just wanted some exercise," said Jip. "Wouldn't you want to stretch your legs if you'd been shut up in a box all day? Probably his home is near here, and that's why he's come back."

"But why," I asked, "did he go the whole way round the mountain first?"

Then Chee-Chee, Polynesia, Jip, and I sat down to rest. Suddenly the Doctor called out:

"Look, look!"

We turned and found that he was pointing to the Jabizri, who was now walking *up* the mountain at a much faster and more businesslike gait.

"Well," said Jip, "if he is going to walk *over* the mountain and back, for more exercise, I'll wait for him here. Chee-Chee and Polynesia can follow him."

Indeed it would have taken a monkey or a bird to climb the place which the beetle was now walking up. It was a smooth, flat part of the mountain's side, steep as a wall.

But presently, when the Jabizri was no more than ten feet above our heads, we all cried out together. For even while we watched him, he had disappeared into the face of the rock, like a raindrop soaking into sand.

"He's gone!" cried Polynesia. "There must be a hole up there." And in a twinkling she had fluttered up the rock and was clinging to the face of it with her claws.

"Yes," she shouted down, "we've run him to earth at last. His hole is right here, behind a patch of lichen — big enough to get two fingers in."

"Ah," cried the Doctor, "this great slab of rock then must have slid down from the summit and shut off the mouth of the cave like a door. Poor fellows! What a dreadful time they must have spent in there! I wonder how thick it is," and he picked up a big stone and banged it with all his might against the face of the rock. It made a hollow booming sound, like a giant drum. We all stood still listening while the echo of it died slowly away.

And then a cold shiver ran down my spine. For, from within the mountain, back came three answering knocks: *Boom! . . . Boom! . . . Boom!*

Wide-eyed we looked at one another as though the earth itself had spoken. And the solemn little silence that followed was broken by the Doctor.

"Thank heaven," he said in a hushed, reverent voice, "some of them at least are alive!"

A Great Moment

THE NEXT PART OF OUR PROBLEM was the hard-
est of all: how to roll aside, pull down, or break
open that gigantic slab. As we gazed up at it towering above our heads, it looked indeed a hopeless
task for our tiny strength.

Chee-Chee scaled up the sheer wall of the slab

and examined the top of it, where it leaned against the mountain's side. I uprooted bushes and stripped off hanging creepers that might conceal a weak place. The Doctor got more leaves and composed new picture letters for the Jabizri to take in if he should turn up again, while Polynesia carried up a handful of nuts and pushed them into the beetle's hole, one by one, for the prisoners inside to eat.

"Nuts are so nourishing," she said.

But Jip it was who, scratching at the foot of the slab like a good ratter, made the discovery which led to our final success.

"Doctor," he cried, running up to John Dolittle with his nose all covered with black mud, "this slab is resting on nothing but a bed of soft earth. If we can only scratch the earth-bed away from under, the slab might drop a little. Then maybe the Indians can climb out over the top."

The Doctor hurried to examine the place where Jip had dug.

"Why, yes," he said, "if we can get the earth away from under this front edge, the slab is standing up so straight, we might even make it fall right down in this direction. It's well worth trying. Let's get at it, quick."

We had no tools but the sticks and slivers of stone which we could find around. A strange sight we must have looked, the whole crew of us squatting down on our heels, scratching and burrowing at the foot of the mountain, like five badgers in a row.

After about an hour, during which in spite of the cold the sweat fell from our foreheads in all directions, the Doctor said,

"Be ready to jump from under, clear out of the way, if she shows signs of moving. If this slab falls on anybody, it will squash him flatter than a pancake."

Presently there was a grating, grinding sound.

"Look out!" yelled John Dolittle. "Here she comes! — Scatter!"

We ran for our lives, outward, toward the sides. The big rock slid gently down, and as I looked upward, I saw the top coming very slowly away from the mountainside. We had unbalanced it below. Faster and faster the top swung forward, downward. Then, with a roaring crash which shook the whole mountain range beneath our feet, it struck the earth and cracked in halves.

The gloomy black mouth of a tunnel, full twenty feet high, was revealed. In the center of this opening stood an enormous Red Indian, seven feet tall, handsome, muscular, slim, and naked — but for a beaded cloth about his middle and an eagle's feather in his hair. He held one hand across his face to shield his eyes from the blinding sun which he had not seen in many days.

"It is he!" I heard the Doctor whisper at my elbow. "I know him by his great height and the scar upon his chin."

And he stepped forward slowly across the fallen stone, with his hand outstretched to the red man.

Presently the Indian uncovered his eyes. And I saw that they had a curious piercing gleam in them — like the eyes of an eagle, but kinder and more gentle. He slowly raised his right arm, the rest of him still and motionless like a statue, and took the Doctor's hand in his. It was a great moment. Polynesia nodded to me in a knowing, satisfied kind of way.

Then the Doctor tried to speak to Long Arrow. But the Indian knew no English, of course, and the Doctor knew no Indian. Presently, to my surprise, I heard the Doctor trying him in the language of eagles.

"Great Redskin," he said in the fierce screams

102

and short grunts that the big birds use, "never have I been so glad in all my life as I am today to find you still alive."

In a flash, Long Arrow's stony face lit up with a smile of understanding, and back came the answer in eagle tongue.

"Mighty White Man, I owe my life to you. For the remainder of my days I am your servant to command," said Long Arrow.

Travelers who have since visited Spidermonkey Island tell me that the huge stone slab is now one of the regular sights of the island. And that the Indian guides, when showing it to visitors, always tell *their* story of how it came there. They say that when the Doctor found that the rocks had entrapped his friend, Long Arrow, he was so angry that he ripped the mountain in halves with his bare hands and let him out.

On the way to the village, some Indians met us and told Long Arrow something which appeared to be sad news, for on hearing it his face grew very grave. The Doctor asked him what was wrong. And Long Arrow said he had just been informed that the chief of the tribe, an old man of eighty, had died early that morning.

"That," Polynesia whispered in my ear, "must have been what they went back to the village for, when the messenger fetched them from the beach. Remember?"

"What did he die of?" asked the Doctor.

"He died of cold," said Long Arrow.

Indeed, now that the sun was setting, we were all shivering ourselves.

"This is a serious thing," said the Doctor to me. "The island is still in the grip of that wretched current flowing southward. We will have to look into this tomorrow. If nothing can be done about it, the Indians had better take to canoes and leave the island. The chance of being wrecked will be better than getting frozen to death in the ice floes of the Antarctic."

Presently we came over a saddle in the hills, and looking downward on the far side of the island, we saw the village — a large cluster of grass huts and gaily colored totem poles close by the edge of the sea.

"How artistic!" said the Doctor. "Delightfully situated. What is the name of the village?"

"Popsipetel," said Long Arrow. "That is the name also of the tribe. The word signifies in Indian tongue, 'The Men of the Moving Land.'"

As Long Arrow took us around the island, we found that not only the plants and trees were suffering from the cold; the animal life was even in worse straits.

Everywhere shivering birds were to be seen, their feathers all fluffed out, gathering together for flight to summer lands. And many lay dead upon the ground. Going down to the shore, we watched land crabs in large numbers taking to the sea to find some better home. While away to the southeast, we could see many icebergs floating — a sign that we were now not far from the terrible region of the Antarctic.

As we were looking out to sea, we noticed our friends the porpoises jumping through the waves. The Doctor hailed them, and they came inshore.

He asked them how far we were from the South Polar Continent.

About a hundred miles, they told him. And then they asked why he wanted to know.

"Because this floating island we are on," said he, "is drifting southward all the time in a current. It's an island that ordinarily belongs somewhere in the tropic zone — real sultry weather, sunstrokes and all that. If it doesn't stop going southward pretty soon, everything on it is going to perish."

"Well," said the porpoises, "then the thing to do is to get it back into a warmer climate, isn't it?"

"Yes, but how?" said the Doctor. "We can't *row* it back."

"No," said they, "but whales could push it — if only you got enough of them."

"What a splendid idea! — Whales, the very thing!" said the Doctor. "Do you think you could get me some?"

"Why, certainly," said the porpoises. "We passed one herd of them out there, sporting about among the icebergs. We'll ask them to come over. And if they aren't enough, we'll try and hunt up some more. Better have plenty."

"Thank you," said the Doctor. "You are very kind. By the way, do you happen to know how this island came to be a floating island? At least half of it, I notice, is made of stone. It is very odd that it floats at all, isn't it?"

"It is unusual," they said. "But the explanation is quite simple. It used to be a mountainous part of South America — an overhanging part — sort of an awkward corner, you might say. Way back in the glacial days, thousands of years ago, it broke off from the mainland; and by some curious accident the inside of it, which is hollow, got filled with air as it fell into the ocean. You can only see less than half of the island: the bigger half is under water. And in the middle of it, underneath, is a huge rock air chamber, running right up inside the mountains. And that's what keeps it floating."

"What a curious phenomenon," said the Doctor. "I must make a note of that." And out came the everlasting notebook.

The porpoises went bounding off toward the icebergs. And not long after, we saw the sea heaving and frothing as a big herd of whales came toward us at full speed.

They certainly were enormous creatures; and there must have been a good two hundred of them.

"Here they are," said the porpoises, poking their heads out of the water.

"Good!" said the Doctor. "Now ask them if they will be so good as to go down to the far end of the island, put their noses against it, and push it back near the coast of Southern Brazil."

Then we lay down upon the beach and waited.

After about an hour the Doctor got up and threw a stick into the water. For a while this floated motionless. But soon we saw it begin to move gently down the coast.

"Ah!" said the Doctor. "See that? — The island is going north at last. Thank goodness!"

The Doctor took out his watch, threw more sticks into the water, and made a rapid calculation.

"Humph! — Fourteen and a half knots an hour," he murmured — "A very nice speed. It should take us about five days to get back near Brazil. Well. that's that — Quite a load off my mind. I declare I feel warmer already. Let's go and get something to eat."

The Whispering Rocks

As usual, the Doctor was kept busy caring for sick Popsipetel babies, monkeys with runny noses, and all manner of ailments the animals and the people of the island brought to him to cure.

One day, when he had finished with all his patients, we went for a complete trip round the island's shores by canoe.

Shortly after we started, while still off the lower end of the island, we sighted a steep point on the coast where the sea was in a great state of turmoil, white with soapy froth. On going nearer, we found that this was caused by our friendly whales, who were still faithfully working away with their noses against the end of the island, driving us northward. Here and there we noticed that the trees on the shore already looked greener and more healthy. Spidermonkey Island was getting back into her home climate.

About halfway to Popsipetel, we went ashore and spent two or three days exploring the central part of the island. Our Indian paddlers took us up into the mountains, very steep and high in this region, overhanging the sea. And they showed us what they called the Whispering Rocks.

This was a very peculiar and striking piece of scenery. It was like a great vast basin, or circus, in the mountains, and out of the center of it there rose a table of rock with an ivory chair upon it.

We asked our guides why it was called the Whispering Rocks, and they said, "Go down into it and we will show you."

The great bowl was miles deep and miles wide.

We scrambled down the rocks, and they showed us how, even when you stood far, far apart from one another, you merely had to whisper in that great place and everyone in the theater could hear you.

Our guides told us that it was here, in days long gone by when the Popsipetels owned the whole of Spidermonkey Island, that the kings were crowned.

They showed us also an enormous hanging stone perched on the edge of a volcano's crater — the highest summit in the whole island. Although it was very far below us, we could see it quite plainly; and it looked wobbly enough to be pushed off its perch with the hand. There was a legend among the people, they said, that when the greatest of all Popsipetel kings should be crowned in the ivory chair, this hanging stone would tumble into the volcano's mouth and go straight down to the center of the earth.

The Doctor said he would like to go and examine it closer.

And when we were come to the lip of the volcano (it took us half a day to get up to it), we found the stone was unbelievably large — big as a cathedral. Underneath it we could look right down into a black hole which seemed to have no bottom. The Doctor explained to us that volcanoes sometimes spurted up fire from these holes in their tops, but that those on floating islands were always cold and dead.

"Stubbins," he said, looking up at the great stone towering above us, "do you know what would most likely happen if that boulder should fall in?"

"No," said I, "what?"

"You remember the air chamber which the porpoises told us lies under the center of the island?"

"Yes."

."Well, this stone is heavy enough, if it fell into the volcano, to break through into that air chamber from above. And once it did, the air would escape and the floating island would float no more. It would sink."

"But then everybody on it would be drowned, wouldn't they?" I asked.

"Oh no, not necessarily, Stubbins. That would depend on the depth of the sea where the sinking took place. The island might touch bottom when it had only gone down, say a hundred feet. But there would be lots of it still sticking up above the water then, wouldn't there?"

"Yes," I replied, "I suppose there would."

We returned to Popsipetel just as the dawn was breaking, and as soon as the Doctor had paid a visit to Long Arrow and seen that he was doing nicely, we proceeded to our own house at the far end of the village. Here we ate some breakfast and then lay down to take a good rest.

Rest, indeed, we needed; for life had been strenuous and busy for us ever since we had landed on the island. And it wasn't many minutes after our weary heads struck the pillows that the whole crew of us were sound asleep.

We were awakened by music. The glaring noon-day sunlight was streaming in at our door, outside of which some kind of a band appeared to be playing. We got up and looked out. Our house was surrounded by the whole population of Popsipetel. We were used to having quite a number of curious and admiring Indians waiting at our door at all hours; but this was quite different. The vast crowd was dressed in its best clothes. Bright beads, gawdy feathers, and gay blankets gave cheerful color to the scene. Everyone seemed in very good humor, singing or playing on musical instruments — mostly painted wooden whistles or drums made from skins.

We found Polynesia sitting on our doorpost, watching the show.

"The result of the election has just been announced," said she. "The name of the new chief was given out at noon."

"And who is the new chief?" asked the Doctor.

"You are," said Polynesia quietly.

"*I!*" gasped the Doctor — "Well, of all things!"

"Yes," said she, "you're the one. And what's more, they've changed your surname for you. They didn't think that Dolittle was a proper or respectful name for a man who had done so much. So you are now to be known as Jong Thinkalot. How do you like it?"

"But I don't *want* to be a chief," said the Doctor in an irritable voice.

"I'm afraid you'll have hard work to get out of it now," said she, "unless you're willing to put to sea again in one of their rickety canoes. You see you've been elected not merely the chief of the Popsipetels; you're to be a king — the king of the whole of Spidermonkey Island."

"Oh, Lord!" groaned the Doctor, "I do wish

they wouldn't be so enthusiastic! Bother it, I don't
want to be a king!"

"I should think, Doctor," said I, "you'd feel
rather proud and glad. I wish *I* had a chance to be
a king."

"Oh, I know it sounds grand," said he, pulling
on his boots miserably. "But the trouble is, you
can't take up responsibilities and then just drop
them again when you feel like it. I have my own
work to do. Scarcely one moment have I had to
give to natural history since I landed on this island.
I've been doing someone else's business all the
time. And now they want me to go on doing it!
Why, once I'm made king of the Popsipetels, that's
the end of me as a useful naturalist. I'd be too busy
for anything. All I'd be then is just a, er — er —
just a king."

"Look," said Polynesia, "here come the head
men to announce your election. Hurry up and get
your boots laced."

⁵ The throng before our door had suddenly parted
asunder, making a long lane; and down this we
now saw a group of personages coming toward us.
The man in front, a handsome old Indian with a
wrinkled face, carried in his hands a wooden

115

crown — a truly beautiful and gorgeous crown, even though of wood. Behind the old man came eight strong Indians bearing a litter.

When the old Indian told John Dolittle that he had come to take him to his coronation, the Doctor politely begged to be excused from the honor, but the old man paid no attention.

"You are the chosen one," said he. "The people will have none but you."

Into the Doctor's perplexed face suddenly there came a flash of hope.

"I'll go and see Long Arrow," he whispered to me. "Perhaps he will know of some way to get me out of this."

And asking the personages to excuse him a moment, he left them there, standing at his door, and hurried off in the direction of Long Arrow's house. I followed him.

We found our big friend lying on a grass bed outside his home, where he had been moved that he might witness the holiday-making.

"Long Arrow," said the Doctor, speaking quickly in eagle tongue so that the bystanders should not overhear, "in dire peril I come to you for help. These men would make me their king. If such a thing befall me, all the great work I hoped to do must go undone, for who is there unfreer than a king? I pray you speak with them and persuade their kind, well-meaning hearts that what they plan to do would be unwise"

Long Arrow raised himself upon his elbow.

"Oh, Kindly One," said he (this seemed now to have become the usual manner of address when speaking to the Doctor), "sorely it grieves me that the first wish you ask of me I should be unable to grant. Alas! I can do nothing. These people have so set their hearts on keeping you for king that if I tried to interfere, they would drive me from their land and likely crown you in the end in any case. A king you must be, if only for a while. We must so arrange the business of governing that you may have time to give to nature's secrets. Later we may be able to hit upon some plan to relieve you of the burden of the crown. But for now you must be king. These people are a headstrong tribe, and they will have their way. There is no other course."

Sadly the Doctor turned away from the bed and faced about. And there behind him stood the old man again, the crown still held in his wrinkled hands and the royal litter waiting at his elbow. With a deep reverence the bearers motioned toward the seat of the chair, inviting the white man to get in.

He turned back pleadingly again to Long Arrow in a last appeal for help. But the big Indian merely shook his head and pointed, like the bearers, to the waiting chair.

At last, almost in tears, John Dolittle stepped slowly into the litter and sat down. As he was hoisted on to the broad shoulders of the bearers, I heard him still feebly muttering beneath his breath, "Botheration take it! — I don't *want* to be a king!"

"Farewell!" called Long Arrow from his bed, "and may good fortune ever stand within the shadow of your throne!"

"He comes! — He comes!" murmured the crowd. "Away! Away! To the Whispering Rocks!"

And as the procession formed up to leave the village, the crowd about us began hurrying off in the direction of the mountains, to make sure of good seats in the giant theater where the crowning ceremony would take place.

The Coronation of King Jong

As Chee-Chee, Polynesia, Jip, and I finally reached the dizzy edge of the great bowl and looked down inside it, it was like gazing over a never-ending ocean of copper-colored faces. For every seat in the theater was filled; every man, woman, and child on the island — including Long Arrow, who had been carried up on his sick bed — was there to see the show.

Soon we saw the royal litter, with the Doctor seated in it, slowly ascending the winding steps of the table. Reaching the flat top at last, it halted, and the Doctor stepped out upon a carpet of flowers. So still and perfect was the silence that even at that distance above I distinctly heard a twig snap beneath his tread.

Walking to the throne accompanied by the old Indian, the Doctor got up upon the stand and sat down. How tiny his little round figure looked when seen from that tremendous height! The throne had been made for longer-legged kings; and when the Doctor was seated, his feet did not reach the ground, but dangled six inches from the top step.

Then the old man turned round, and looking up at the people, began to speak in a quiet, even voice; but every word he said was easily heard in the farthest corner of the Whispering Rocks.

First he recited the names of all the great Popsipetel kings who in days long ago had been crowned in this ivory chair. He spoke of the greatness of the Popsipetel people, of their triumphs, of their hardships. Then waving his hand toward the Doctor, he began recounting the things which this king-to-be had done. And I am bound to say that they easily outmatched the deeds of those who had gone before him.

At last the old man finished his speech, and stepping up to the chair, very respectfully removed the Doctor's battered high hat. He was about to put it upon the ground, but the Doctor took it from him hastily and kept it on his lap. Then taking up the sacred crown he placed it upon John Dolittle's head. It did not fit very well (for it had been made for smaller-headed kings), and when the wind blew in freshly from the sunlit sea the Doctor had some difficulty in keeping it on. But it looked very splendid.

Turning once more to the people, the old man said, "Men of Popsipetel, behold your elected king! — Are you content?"

And then at last the voice of the people broke loose.

"JONG! JONG!" they shouted. "Long live KING JONG!"

The sound burst upon the solemn silence with the crash of a hundred cannon. There, where even a whisper carried miles, the shock of it was like a blow in the face.

Suddenly I saw the old man point upward, to the highest mountain in the island; and looking over my shoulder, I was just in time to see the hanging stone topple slowly out of sight — down into the heart of the volcano.

"See ye, Men of the Moving Land!" the old man cried: "The stone has fallen and our legend has come true: the King of Kings is crowned this day!"

The Doctor too had seen the stone fall and he was now standing up looking at the sea expectantly.

"He's thinking of the air chamber," said Polynesia in my ear. "Let us hope that the sea isn't very deep in these parts."

After a full minute (so long did it take the stone to fall that depth) we heard a muffled, distant, crunching thud — and then, immediately after, a great hissing of escaping air. The Doctor, his face tense with anxiety, sat down in the throne again, still watching the blue water of the ocean with staring eyes.

Soon we felt the island slowly sinking beneath us. We saw the sea creep inland over the beaches as the shores went down — one foot, three feet, ten feet, twenty, fifty, a hundred. And then, thank goodness, gently as a butterfly alighting on a rose, it stopped! Spidermonkey Island had come to rest on the sandy bottom of the Atlantic, and earth was joined to earth once more.

Of course many of the houses near the shores were now under water. Popsipetel Village itself had entirely disappeared. But it didn't matter. No one was drowned, for every soul in the island was high up in the hills watching the coronation of King Jong.

In Popsipetel history the story was handed down (and it is firmly believed to this day) that when King Jong sat upon the throne, so great was his mighty weight that the very island itself sank down to do him honor, and never moved again.

The Sea Serpent

LIFE IN SPIDERMONKEY ISLAND went forward month in month out, busily and pleasantly. The winter, with Christmas celebrations, came and went, and summer was with us once again before we knew it.

As time passed, the Doctor became more and more taken up with the care of his big family;

and the hours he could spare for his natural history work grew fewer and fewer. I knew that he often still thought of his house and garden in Puddleby, and of his plans and ambitions; because once in a while we would notice his face grow thoughtful and a little sad, when something reminded him of England or his old life. But he never spoke of these things. And I truly believe he would have spent the remainder of his days on Spidermonkey Island if it hadn't been for an accident — and for Polynesia.

It was a perfect Popsipetel day, bright and hot, blue and yellow. Drowsily I looked out to sea, thinking of my mother and father. I wondered if they were getting anxious over my long absence. Beside me old Polynesia went on grumbling away in low steady tones, and her words began to mingle and mix with the gentle lapping of the waves upon the shore. It may have been the even murmur of her voice, helped by the soft and balmy air, that lulled me to sleep. I don't know. Anyhow I presently dreamed that the island had moved again — not floatingly as before, but suddenly, jerkily, as though something enormously powerful had heaved it up from its bed just once and let it down.

How long I slept after that I have no idea. I was awakened by a gentle pecking on the nose.

"Tommy! — Tommy!" (It was Polynesia's voice.) "Wake *up!* — Gosh, what a boy, to sleep through an earthquake and never notice it! — Tommy, listen: here's our chance now. Wake *up,* for goodness' sake!"

"What's the matter?" I asked, sitting up with a yawn.

"Sh! — Look!" whispered Polynesia, pointing out to sea.

Still only half awake, I stared before me with bleary, sleep-laden eyes. And in the shallow water, not more than thirty yards from shore, I saw an enormous pale pink shell. Dome-shaped, it towered up in a graceful rainbow curve to a tremendous height; and round its base the surf broke gently in little waves of white. It could have belonged to the wildest dream.

"What in the world is it?" I asked.

"That," whispered Polynesia, "is what sailors for hundreds of years have called the 'Sea Serpent.' I've seen it myself more than once from the decks of ships, at long range, curving in and out of the water. But now that I see it close and still, I very strongly suspect that the Sea Serpent of history is no other than the legendary Great Glass Sea Snail. If that isn't the only fish of its kind in the seven seas, call me a carrion crow. Tommy, we're in luck. Our job is to get the Doctor down here to look at that prize specimen before it moves off to the Deep Hole. If we can, then trust me, we may leave this blessed island yet. You stay here and keep an eye on it, while I go after the Doctor. Don't move or speak — don't even breathe heavy. He might get scared — awful timid things, snails. Just watch him, and I'll be back in two shakes."

It moved very little. From time to time it would try to draw itself up, the way a snail does when he goes to move, but almost at once it would sink down again, as if exhausted. It seemed to me to act as though it were hurt underneath; but the lower part of it, which was below the level of the water, I could not see.

I was still absorbed in watching the great beast when Polynesia returned with the Doctor. They approached so silently and so cautiously that I neither saw nor heard them coming till I found them crouching beside me on the sand.

One sight of the snail changed the Doctor completely. His eyes just sparkled with delight. I had not seen him so thrilled and happy since the time we caught the Jabizri beetle when we first landed on the island.

"It is he!" he whispered — "The Great Glass Sea Snail himself — not a doubt of it. Polynesia, go down the shore a way and see if you can find any of the porpoises for me. Perhaps they can tell us what the snail is doing here — It's very unusual for him to be in shallow water like this. And Stubbins, you go over to the harbor and bring me a small canoe. But be most careful how you paddle it round into this bay. If the snail should take fright and go out into the deeper water, we may never get a chance to see him again."

"And don't tell any of the Indians," Polynesia added in a whisper, as I moved to go. "We must keep this a secret, or we'll have a crowd of sightseers round here in five minutes. It's mighty lucky we found the snail in a quiet bay."

Reaching the harbor, I picked out a small light canoe from among the number that were lying there, and without telling anyone what I wanted it for, got in and started off to paddle it down the shore.

Polynesia, I saw, when I rounded a rocky cape

and came in sight of the bay, had got her errand done and returned ahead of me, bringing with her a pair of porpoises. These were already conversing in low tones with John Dolittle. I beached the canoe and went up to listen.

"What I want to know," the Doctor was saying, "is how the snail comes to be here. I was given to understand that he usually stayed in the Deep Hole, and that when he did come to the surface, it was always in mid-ocean."

"Oh, didn't you know? Haven't you heard?" the porpoises replied. "You covered up the Deep Hole when you sank the island. Why yes: you let it down right on top of the mouth of the Hole — sort of put the lid on, as it were. The fishes that were in it at the time have been trying to get out ever since. The Great Snail had the worst luck of all: the island nipped him by the tail just as he was leaving the Hole for a quiet evening stroll. And he was held there for six months, trying to wriggle himself free. Finally he had to heave the whole island up at one end to get his tail loose. Didn't you feel a sort of an earthquake shock about an hour ago?"

"Yes, I did," said the Doctor.

"Well, that was the snail heaving up the island

to get out of the Hole," they said. "All the other fishes saw their chance, and escaped when he raised the lid. It was lucky for them he's so big and strong. But the strain of that terrific heave told on him; he sprained a muscle in his tail, and it started swelling rather badly. He wanted some quiet place to rest up, and seeing this soft beach handy, he crawled in here."

"Dear me!" said the Doctor. "I'm terribly sorry. I suppose I should have given some sort of notice that the island was going to be let down. But, to tell the truth, we didn't know it ourselves; it happened by a kind of an accident. Do you imagine the poor fellow is hurt very badly?"

"We're not sure," said the porpoises, "because none of us can speak his language. But we swam right around him on our way in here, and he did not seem to be really seriously injured."

"Can't any of your people speak shellfish?" the Doctor asked.

"Not a word," said they. "It's a most frightfully difficult language."

"Do you think that you might be able to find me some kind of a fish that could?"

"We don't know," said the porpoises. "We might try."

130

"I should be extremely grateful to you if you would," said the Doctor. "There are many important questions I want to ask this snail. And besides, I would like to do my best to cure his tail for him. It's the least I can do. After all, it was my fault, indirectly, that he got hurt."

"Well, if you wait here," said the porpoises, "we'll see what can be done."

Shellfish Language at Last

MANY AND CURIOUS WERE THE CREATURES they produced. First they found a sea urchin (a funny ball-like little fellow with long whiskers all over him) who said he couldn't speak Shellfish, but knew starfish language well enough. Then they located a starfish who could speak Shellfish moderately well.

Feeling quite encouraged, the Doctor and I, with the porpoises, the urchin, and the starfish swimming alongside, paddled the canoe close to the shell of the Great Snail.

And then began the most curious conversation I have ever witnessed. First the starfish would ask the snail something; and whatever answer the snail gave, the starfish would tell it to the sea urchin, the urchin would tell it to the porpoises, and the porpoises would tell it to the Doctor.

After this had gone on for some time, the Doctor leaned over the edge of the canoe and put his face below the water, to try to follow the strange conversation more closely.

Hours went by, but little by little he found that he was succeeding.

"Stubbins," he said, lifting his face from the water for the hundredth time, "I'm beginning to converse directly with the Great Snail. I've managed to convey to him that I think he would be better on a dry part of the beach where I can examine his tail. Will you please go back to town and get my medicine bag?"

This time when I got back to the shore with the medicine bag, I found the snail high and dry on the beach. John Dolittle was examining a swelling on his tail.

From the bag which I had brought, the Doctor took a large bottle of embrocation and began rubbing the sprain. Next, he took all the bandages he had in the bag and fastened them end to end. With this he got the sprain strapped to his satisfaction.

The snail really seemed to be quite pleased with the attention he had received, and he stretched himself in lazy comfort when the Doctor was done. In this position, when the shell on his back was empty, you could look right through it and see the palm trees on the other side.

The Doctor seemed very tired. On the way back to the palace, Polynesia said, "Doctor, you ought to take a holiday. All kings take holidays once in a while — every one of them."

The Doctor made no reply, and we walked on silently toward the town. I could see, nevertheless, that her words had made an impression on him.

After supper, he disappeared from the palace without saying where he was going — a thing he had never done before. Of course we all knew where he had gone: back to the beach to sit up with the snail.

When he had gone, Polynesia called us together

and said, "Look here, you fellows, we've simply got to get the Doctor to take this holiday some-how — unless we're willing to stay on this blessed island for the rest of our lives."

"But what difference," I asked, "is his taking a holiday going to make?"

Impatiently Polynesia turned to me and said:

"Don't you see? If he has a clear week to get thoroughly interested in his natural history again — marine stuff, his dream of seeing the floor of the ocean, and all that — there may be some chance of his consenting to leave this pesky place. But while he is here on duty as king, he never gets a moment to think of anything outside of the busi-ness of government."

"Yes, that's true. He's far too conscientious," I said.

"And besides," Polynesia went on, "his only hope of ever getting away from here would be to leave secretly. Why, I believe if they thought he had any idea of escaping, they would put chains on him."

"Yes, I really think they would," I agreed. "Yet without a ship of some kind I don't see how the Doctor is going to get away, even secretly."

"Well, I'll tell you," said Polynesia. "If we do

succeed in making him take this holiday, our next step will be to get the sea snail to promise to take us all in his shell and carry us to the mouth of Puddleby River. If we can once get the snail willing, the temptation will be too much for John Dolittle, and he'll come, I know — especially as he'll be able to take those new plants and drugs of Long Arrow's to the English doctors, as well as see the floor of the ocean on the way."

"How thrilling!" I cried. "Do you mean the snail could take us under the sea all the way back to Puddleby?"

"Certainly," said Polynesia, "a little trip like that is nothing to him. He would crawl along the floor of the ocean and the Doctor could see all the sights. Perfectly simple. Oh, John Dolittle will come all right, if we can only get him to take that holiday — *and* if the snail will consent to give us the ride."

"Golly, I hope he does!" sighed Jip. "I'm sick of these beastly tropics; they make you feel so lazy and good-for-nothing. And there are no rats or anything here — not that a fellow would have the energy to chase 'em even if there were. My, wouldn't I be glad to see old Puddleby and the garden again! And won't Dab-Dab be glad to have us back!"

Well, you can guess how glad we were when next morning the Doctor, after his all-night conversation with the snail, told us that he had made up his mind to take the holiday.

Polynesia was immensely pleased. She at once set quietly to work making arrangements for our departure, taking good care the while that no one should get an inkling of where we were going, what we were taking with us, the hour of our leaving, or which of the palace gates we would go out by.

Long Arrow, who was the only Indian let into the secret of our destination, said he would like to come with us as far as the beach to see the Great Snail; and him Polynesia told to be sure and bring his collection of plants.

Midnight, the hour when most of the townspeople would be asleep and the Doctor would be down on the beach sitting up with his patient, she finally chose for our departure.

We had to take a week's food supply with us for the royal holiday. So, with our other packages, we were heavy-laden when on the stroke of twelve we opened the west door of the palace and stepped cautiously and quietly into the moonlit garden. I gently closed the heavy door behind us.

On our arrival at the beach, we found the snail already feeling much better and now able to move his tail without pain.

The porpoises (who are by nature inquisitive creatures) were still hanging about in the offing to see if anything of interest was going to happen. Polynesia, the plotter, while the Doctor was occupied with his new patient, signaled to them and drew them aside for a little private chat.

"Now see here, my friends," said she speaking low, "you know how much John Dolittle has done for the animals — given his whole life up to them, one might say. Well, here is your chance to do something for him. Listen: if this snail were only willing to take him and us, and a little baggage — not very much: thirty or forty pieces, say — inside his shell and carry us to England, we feel sure that the Doctor would go, because he's just crazy to mess about on the floor of the ocean. Now it is highly important that the Doctor return to his own country to carry on his proper work, which means such a lot to the animals of the world. So what we want you to do is to tell the sea urchin to tell the starfish to tell the snail to take us in his shell and carry us to Puddleby River. Is that plain?"

"Quite, quite," said the porpoises. "And we will willingly do our very best to persuade him."

John Dolittle, unaware of anything save the work he was engaged on, was standing knee-deep in the shallow water, helping the snail try out his mended tail, to see if it were well enough to travel on.

Half an hour passed.

What success the porpoises had met with, we did not know, till suddenly the Doctor left the snail's side and came splashing out to us, quite breathless.

"What *do* you think?" he cried. "While I was talking to the snail just now, he offered, of his own accord, to take us all back to England inside his shell. He says he has got to go on a voyage of discovery anyway, to hunt up a new home, now that the Deep Hole is closed. Said it wouldn't be much out of his way to drop us at Puddleby River, if we cared to come along — Goodness, what a chance! I'd love to go. To examine the floor of the ocean all the way from Brazil to Europe! No man ever did it before. What a glorious trip — Oh, that I had never allowed myself to be made king! Now I must see the chance of a lifetime slip by."

Out of the darkness at my elbow, Polynesia rose and quietly moved down to his side.

"Now, Doctor," said she in a soft persuasive voice, as though she were talking to a wayward child, "you know this king business is not your real work in life. These natives will be able to get along without you. The work you'll do, the information you'll carry home, will be of far more value than what you're doing here."

"Good friend," said the Doctor turning to her sadly, "I cannot leave them now."

"That's where you're wrong, Doctor," said she. "Now is when you should go. The longer you stay, the harder it will be to leave — Go now. Go to-night."

"What, steal away without even saying good-bye to them? Why Polynesia, what a thing to suggest!"

"A fat chance they would give you to say good-bye!" snorted Polynesia, growing impatient at last. "I tell you, Doctor, if you go back to that palace tonight, for good-byes or anything else, you will stay there. Now — this moment — is the time for you to go."

The truth of the old parrot's words seemed to be striking home, for the Doctor stood silent a minute, thinking.

140

"But there are the notebooks," he said presently. "I would have to go back to fetch them."

"I have them here, Doctor," said I, speaking up — "all of them."

Again he pondered.

"And Long Arrow's collection," he said. "I would have to take that also with me."

"It is here, oh Kindly One," came the Indian's deep voice from the shadow beneath the palm.

"But what about provisions," asked the Doctor — "food for the journey?"

"We have a week's supply with us, for our holiday," said Polynesia — "that's more than we will need."

"And then there's my hat," he said fretfully at last. "That settles it: I'll *have* to go back to the palace. I can't leave without my hat. How could I appear in Puddleby with this crown on my head?"

"Here it is, Doctor," said I, producing the hat, old, battered, and beloved, from under my coat.

Polynesia had indeed thought of everything.

Yet even now we could see the Doctor was still trying to think up further excuses.

"Oh, Kindly One," said Long Arrow, "why tempt ill fortune? Your way is clear. Your future and your work beckon you back to your foreign home beyond the sea. With you will go also what lore I too have gathered for mankind — to lands where it will be of wider use than it can ever be here. I see the glimmerings of dawn in the eastern heaven. Day is at hand. Go before your subjects are abroad. Go before your project is discovered. For truly I believe that if you go not now, you will linger the remainder of your days a captive king in Popsipetel."

Great decisions often take no more than a moment in the making. Against the now paling sky I saw the Doctor's figure suddenly stiffen. Slowly he lifted the sacred crown from off his head and laid it on the sands.

And when he spoke, his voice was choked with tears.

"They will find it here," he murmured, "when they come to search for me. And they will know that I have gone. . . . My children, my poor children! — I wonder will they ever understand why it was I left them. . . . I wonder will they ever understand — and forgive."

He took his old hat from me; then, facing Long Arrow, gripped his outstretched hand in silence.

"You decide aright, oh Kindly One," said the Indian — "though none will miss and mourn you more than Long Arrow, the son of Golden Arrow. Farewell, and may good fortune ever lead you by the hand!"

It was the first and only time I ever saw the Doctor weep. Without a word to any of us, he turned and moved down the beach into the shallow water of the sea.

The snail humped up its back and made an opening between its shoulders and the edge of its shell. The Doctor clambered up and passed within. We followed him, after handing up the baggage. The opening shut tight with a whistling suction noise.

Then turning in the direction of the east, the great creature began moving smoothly forward, down the slope into the deeper waters.

Just as the swirling dark green surf was closing in above our heads, the big morning sun popped his rim up over the edge of the ocean. And through our transparent walls of pearl we saw the watery world about us suddenly light up with that most wondrously colorful of visions, a daybreak beneath the sea.

WAS DOCTOR DOLITTLE a real person? Not really. But to Hugh Lofting, the author of this book, he was very much alive.

When Hugh Lofting was a soldier during World War I, he was sent far from home. He wrote many letters to his children, Colin and Elizabeth. He did not want to write about the sadness of war. So he made up stories to amuse them.

Hugh Lofting loved animals. He worried about the poor horses who were forced to go into battle. Horses suffered just as men did. They were frightened. Often they were wounded, just as men were. But horses could not speak for themselves. Hugh Lofting thought that the best doctor to treat a sick horse must be a doctor who could understand horse language. And that is how Mr. Lofting invented the great Doctor Dolittle — a doctor who learned to speak to all the animals in their own languages.

Hugh Lofting wrote many letters to Colin and Elizabeth about Doctor Dolittle. When Mr. Lofting came home from the war, he decided to share those stories with other children. His first book about Doctor Dolittle was published in 1920. Children who loved animals, loved the good doctor too. So Mr. Lofting wrote many other books about him.

Since then, millions of children have enjoyed these stories about the kind and funny Doctor Dolittle, who was surely the greatest animal doctor in the world.